I0543172

The Variant

Justin M. Woodward

simple bicycle publishing

This is a work of fiction. The character and events described herein are imaginary and are not intended to refer to specific places or any persons alive or dead. All rights reserved. No part of this publication may be reproduced, distributed, or transmitted in any form or by any means, including photocopying, recording, or electronic or mechanical methods without the prior written permission of the publisher except for brief quotations embodied in critical reviews.

Copyright © 2016 by Justin M. Woodward, simple bicycle publishing

ISBN-13: 978-0-9979409-0-9
ISBN-10: 0-9979409-0-5

Edited by: Alison R. Woodward
Cover art by: Aaron Jones

www.justinmwoodward.com

For Nathan,
who saves me each and every day.

Acknowledgements

I want to start by thanking my beautiful, amazing wife Alison, who provided me all the support and advice I could need, and thank you for doing such a great job editing this book, I love you! Thank you Aaron Jones for bringing the cover art I envisioned in my head to life, you're awesome. Thank you to fellow author, James F. Goffio, your novel, *House of the Holy* inspired me to get back into writing and reading.

Thank you to my family for your support (especially you, mom!). Thank you to Nathan, who inspires me to be a better person every day. And thank YOU for buying this book. I hope you enjoy it as much as I enjoyed writing it.

The Variant

"I'll do anything for you,
Kill anyone for you."
— Coheed and Cambria

"Someday when the pages of my life
end, I know that you will be one of its
most beautiful chapters."
— Unknown

"You want to be good for the ones you
love, because you know that your time with
them will end up being too short, no matter
how long it is."
— Stephen King

PART ONE
Livin' in the Middle

1

Once again, Tyler Roydman rushed into his small office building holding his briefcase over his head. It had been raining for three straight days, and this morning was no exception. Weather like this always made him feel miserable and lethargic. He immediately turned as he entered the building, reaching for the door so that he could hold it open for Anne.

Anne fucking Weaver. The self-righteous bitch.

Anne was the receiver of the new writing job at the paper, the job that Tyler had applied for *weeks* before she had been hired. Fresh off the street, too. He supposed a pretty face and a two-year degree from any second-rate school possibly did matter more than his ten years of service for the company. After all, his card *had* read: *No one edits and writes classified ads quite like you, dickhead!*

Or at least it felt like it had.

Sometimes a punch in the stomach and a certificate for ten years of service doesn't feel so different.

At least there had been cake, even if he didn't eat cake. He had just smiled and gritted his teeth as always. As if he had time, what with all the emails and calls about selling this trampoline, that dog, this shit, that shit.

Someone's trash is someone else's future trash.

But it paid the bills. If only he had a little extra money in his wallet after paying those bills.

His wallet.

It must have fallen out of his pocket when he stepped out of his car on that rainy April morning in Monticello, Minnesota. He figured it wouldn't be so bad getting his wallet out of the rain if his keys weren't in the ignition.

Could things get any worse? He thought.

They could. It was only Monday after all.

2

When Tyler got to his desk he sat down and booted up his 1999 Dell desktop computer. There were ninety-five emails to go through this morning which was pretty average for a Monday. He thought of the line: *Looks like somebody's got a case of the Mondays* from *Office Space* and a smile crept across his face.

At least she doesn't work here, he thought.

When Mr. Sanderfer came around each Monday morning to ask about Tyler's weekend while simultaneously spewing the latest corporate bullshit, Tyler always liked to come up with newer and even more elaborate lies each time. A weekend in Hawaii. Drinks with Mark Zuckerberg. Backstage pass to the Rush concert. Anything which made Mr. Sanderfer's weekend as insignificant as possible by comparison. Also, mainly because he doubted he even listened to his answers.

"I actually got to go film a hunting segment in Canada with my uncle. He's a higher-up at Gander Mountain and they sent us on an all expens-"

"That's great," Mr. Sanderfer said, while looking down at something in his hand. He continued by adding, "Okay, well these papers don't write themselves yah know!" and he walked back into his office, shutting the door behind him.

Tyler didn't even mind the blatant interruption. Mr. Sanderfer was gone, and that was a win in his book. After all, he did *actually* have a whole hour or two's worth of work to do before he could spend the rest of the day pretending he was busy.

But first, he had to break into his own car.

"Knock knock," Tyler said as he knocked on the door to Jimmy's office. Jimmy was one of the editors for the paper, and incidentally, the only person in the office who owned a jimmy. The irony of the situation was not lost on Tyler.

Aside from the whole 'locking the keys in the car' shenanigans, Tyler's day was pretty straightforward. In fact, his entire life had become routine.

Go to work.

Go to the store.

Go home and smoke some weed until passing out.

It wasn't that Tyler didn't have aspirations; he just didn't have any real motivation anymore. Put a gun to his head and he would tell you he wanted to be a writer. He had taken the job at the paper as a stepping stone for his career, straight out of high school in 2005. He was able to go to night classes and get his journalism degree. The paper even helped pay for it. He figured he could work his way up and be a front page columnist by now, but he was still just writing the classified ads. He did have his short stories though. Some of them were actually quite good, but only a select few strangers on the internet had given him the time of day. It's funny how people who don't know you sometimes can be more encouraging than your own friends and family. Tyler found it easier to talk to people who didn't know him anyways, especially after what had happened three years ago.

When Tyler kidnapped his own son.

3

It was July fourth. Tyler's son, Nathan, was spend-
ing the weekend with him. Tyler and Ashleigh had
been separated for almost a year, and Nathan loved
his daddy time. They were on good terms for the
most part, but when Ashleigh found it hard to fully
love Tyler anymore, she decided to do him a favor
and set him free. Her father had been killed in a
work-related accident months prior and she hadn't
been herself since.

Tyler was overcome with excitement when Ashleigh
pulled her car into the driveway on that hot summer
afternoon. He walked outside and slowly crept
around the back of the car in an attempt to surprise
his son. Nathan was turning his head left and right
while his mother undid his car seat straps, trying to
decide where he was. Tyler jumped out from behind the car door.

"NATE MAN!" Tyler shouted.

"Dadeeee!" Nathan answered, with much enthusiasm. Tyler picked up his son and kissed him on the cheek.

"You guys have fun." Ashleigh said. "And try not to catch anything on fire or lose any fingers!"

"Of course!" Tyler yelled as he flew his son around the yard like Buzz Lightyear chasing the evil Emperor Zurg.

Tyler told Nathan to give mommy a kiss and tell her bye-bye, and he did. But then something different happened. Ashleigh leaned towards Tyler and found his lips with her own. They held their kiss for several seconds, after which Ashleigh said "You're a great dad." Tyler smiled and said "I know." His weak attempt at a Han Solo impersonation.

As Ashleigh got in her car, Tyler could tell things were about to get a lot better for them.

But that couldn't be further from the truth.

4

Tyler hated that Ashleigh was unable to get off of work for the weekend. But it was typical. He knew her job had been one of the reasons they had drifted apart. She worked for a big law firm downtown and it had practically consumed her life. She was constantly asked to stay late to work on cases—or pick up Mr. Moore's dry-cleaning—whichever was more pressing at the time.

Tyler was very much looking forward to asking if she would stay and enjoy some fireworks with Nathan and himself this year; but when she told him she was working, he didn't make a big deal out of it. He didn't want her feeling left out. He brought Nathan inside and sat him on the couch, turning on the movie *Cars*. This made it easier to bring all of the bags inside and make some dinner without Nathan clinging to him like a dryer sheet. As Tyler reached for the door to retrieve Nathan's bags from the porch, Nathan cried out, "Orey!"

"Oh yeah!" said Tyler, and he handed Nathan his Orey, a blanket with Eeyore from *Winnie The Pooh* on it. It was one of the tiny blankets with an actual head and arms. Tyler was sure he had heard Ashleigh refer to it as a lovey. It was Nathan's lifeline. They were the best of pals. Orey would take a bullet for Nathan. Nathan would do Orey's taxes for him.

Tyler had told him that he was already two years old and Oreys were for babies, and Nathan had told his daddy to get fucked, only with his eyes rather than his words. Nathan took Orey from Tyler and nodded appreciatively and returned to watching his movie while absentmindedly sucking on the middle two fingers of his left hand.

Tyler got all of Nathan's belongings to his room and began to make dinner for the two of them. After dinner, Tyler showed Nathan the fireworks he had bought. He had several sparklers, some bottle rockets, and one which was called *The Champ*. Linda at *Best Bang In Town* fireworks had told Tyler that it was guaranteed to impress a two year old. Tyler was not sure if that was a hard achievement to accomplish, but he said what the hell, and bought it.

Tyler's parents and Ashleigh's mother came over to enjoy the fireworks with them. Tyler decided to let Nathan hold the sparklers by himself this year after explaining how dangerous they can be if used improperly. Nathan ran around the yard giggling, holding his sparkler as if he had just retrieved the master sword in *The Legend of Zelda*. It made Tyler immensely happy to see Nathan enjoying himself so much. He really loved his son. He would always roll his eyes when people would talk about how 'ya just don't know until ya have yer own,' but it was, in fact, true. From the first time Nathan grabbed his finger in the hospital, he had his whole heart. They shared a kind of special, almost unreal bond.

They chased each other around the yard, enjoying what would be their last night together. It had been a good one. After everyone else had gone home and Tyler had succeeded in impressing a two year old, it was time for bed.

5

Tyler read Nathan a couple of bedtime stories, he told him goodnight, kissed him, and put him in the bed. He turned off the last light in the house, but he left the porch light on. It was a habit he had picked up when Nathan was born. He had developed an irrational fear of someone taking or hurting him, and he felt safer leaving a light on.

He went into his room and sat on his bed. He reached over to the bedside table to grab the remote for the TV. But then he did something he hadn't done in a while. He picked up his iPhone and called Ashleigh, not to ask about their son, but just to talk.

"Hello?" Ashleigh had said after the third ring.

"Hey...What's up?" Tyler asked her.

"I'm just now leaving work. They're going to trial on Monday and you know how they are," she said.

"Yeah, well…Nathan is okay," he wasn't sure why he had said that. He wasn't even sure why he had called.

"Okay...is that all?" Ashleigh said, sounding a bit confused. Tyler wasn't sure if it was all. He told her he would talk to her tomorrow. After they had gotten off of the phone, Tyler set an alarm and went to sleep.

He was in a deep sleep when he heard it. It was a crackle on the baby monitor—the kind of noise he would hear when Nathan was re-adjusting himself in his crib. He sat up in the bed and stared at the baby monitor waiting for the green light to ascend to yellow, and then red. But it stayed green. Everything was fine. He lay back down and closed his eyes. Almost immediately, he heard the thing he hoped he would never hear in the middle of the night—the unmistakable creak of the side rails being let down on Nathan's crib.

"Daddy!" he heard Nathan say through the monitor. But it wasn't a distressed or sad voice. It was a *happy* voice.

Maybe he finally figured out how to let himself out. I knew I should have gotten him a toddler bed by now, Tyler thought, as he got out of bed, sighing.

He was all the way to the doorway of his bedroom when he heard a deep voice traveling through the baby monitor. His heart sank into his chest. Every hair on his body was standing straight up, and his heart felt like it would explode. He reached into his sock drawer and pulled out his pistol—a Glock 17 that his father had given him when he moved out.

Here kid, take this, and try not to shoot anyone unless you really have to.

Tyler turned the handle to the bedroom door to pull it open but it wouldn't budge. He started to panic.

"What the fuck?" he yelled.

He thought about shooting through the door but he didn't want to accidentally shoot his son. He yanked again and again on the door getting more frustrated, more defeated with each pull. He looked under the door to see what he could see—feet— anything.

Nothing.

He backed up as far as he could and flung himself against the door, but right before his body connected with the door—only an inch or so away from the wood—he was flung backwards in a terrible crash onto the bedroom floor. His head was filled with awful thoughts and he could barely keep himself from getting sick. He pulled himself up onto all fours—doggie style, since he was fucked anyways—and reached for the gun. He stood and turned to face the bedroom window. Without thinking, he pointed the gun at the window and pulled the trigger three times.

Shots fired.

He picked up a shirt from the floor and wrapped it around his right hand, using it to punch the remaining glass out of the frame. Tyler then jumped out into the warm, sticky, repulsive night. He circled the house, noticing that all doors were closed, and all lights were off except for his and Nathan's bedrooms.

There Tyler stood in his front yard, wearing nothing but his boxers and wielding a 9mm pistol. The adrenaline coursing through his body was shooting painful spurts of hatred through his spine. He yelled his son's name at the top of his lungs.

"Nathan!!"

Silence.

He could see no headlights in the dark of the night—no tail lights either. He was sure that he would have seen a car leaving, or at least heard one. His road was a long, straight one, and all Tyler could see was black, empty void in both directions. Then he turned and went through the front door, which was unlocked, deadbolt and all. Tyler could see no sign of forced entry anywhere. However, the lamp which usually resided on the small table by the door, now resided on the floor. He walked down the hallway to Nathan's room holding his gun steady about waist high, pointing it at the floor. His breathing was shaky, and the air felt thin and shallow in his lungs. As he peeked around the corner into Nathan's room, he saw what he expected to see—nothing. There was only an empty crib and an empty room. He turned and went back out the front door and made a circle around the house. Defeated, he began to sob deeply as he pulled his iPhone out of his pocket and dialed 9-1-1.

6

The police came and searched Tyler's home and several miles surrounding it extensively. They bombarded him with question after question. They asked about the lamp. Tyler didn't know. They asked about the door refusing to open. Tyler didn't know. They asked about the blood on the front porch. Tyler's whole world seemed to collapse at the last question.

What blood on the porch?

As Detective Dugger was finishing up his interrogation of Tyler, an officer asked him to come outside and see something. Detective Dugger and Tyler followed the young officer outside and around to the back of the house. As they approached the tree line, Tyler saw it. A perfect symmetrical half of an Eeyore lovey—*Nathan's* Eeyore lovey—as if it had been torn in half by a swift katana strike.

"Let me guess Mr. Roydman." Detective Dugger spat. "You don't know about this either."

He didn't.

When Tyler spoke next his voice croaked like someone who had been in a coma for ten years and was just now deciding to start talking again.

"Why are you treating me like I did this?" He demanded. "Like I'm a suspect?"

Detective Dugger spat his dip at Tyler's feet. "Because you *are* a suspect, son," he said.

Ashleigh arrived in just enough time to watch Tyler be shoved into a police car.

It wasn't that Tyler was going to jail, not yet anyways. He had to be questioned more formally, and on video this time. The investigators would find that the blood on the porch was Tyler's. There were no fingerprints, footprints, car tracks, or any piece of evidence whatsoever that didn't belong to Tyler. The investigator found it *interesting* that the deadbolt had been unlocked somehow, and that Tyler's bedroom door magically would not open for him, making it so that he had to shoot out his own window. None of it made sense though. The pieces didn't fit.

Of course, they questioned Ashleigh, too.

A young investigator by the name of Smith brought Ashleigh into a small, cold room and began with the onslaught. He wanted to know about the phone call that had been made the previous night. Ashleigh told him that all Tyler had really said was that Nathan was fine.

"What does that mean?" The young investigator asked. "Why wouldn't he be fine? Was he sick?"

"No..I mean I thought it was strange, but then again, I think he just wanted to talk to me."

"You mean to say that something was troubling him."

Ashleigh could see where this was going.

"Let me be clear," Ashleigh began, "Nathan is Tyler's whole world. He's both of ours. He would never do anything to hurt him."

"Of course not," said Smith, his face solid and unsympathetic. "But if you would, miss, allow *me* to be clear. In a case like this we have to consider all options. And right now we have no evidence to suggest that anyone other than Tyler or yourself entered that house."

7

The disappearance of Nathan Roydman was a huge story. The media had a field day discussing the mystery in gruesome detail. One magazine explained how Tyler had been so distraught over his wife leaving him that he decided to take away her son, dissolving his corpse in acid. Many people believed Tyler was so crazy that he didn't even know what he had done. And it was a damn shame that they let him walk.

The first year was the worst. Angry letters, flaming bags of dog shit on the porch, an elderly woman had told Tyler that he was going to the lowest level of hell as she passed him in the grocery store. Tyler had become so numb to it. At first, he wondered why people had taken the stance that *he* was responsible for his son being missing, or dead, or whatever they believed. But then he had just accepted that the masses believe the media, and the media loved a good father-killed-his-baby story.

Sometimes Tyler even wondered if he *was* crazy.

Ashleigh stood by Tyler at first, but eventually even she couldn't stand to be in the same room as him. It wasn't that she truly believed he had killed Nathan; it was that being around him reminded her that he was never coming back. Tyler, on the other hand, wasn't convinced that Nathan was truly gone. He was willing to accept the fact that it made him 'crazy' by normal standards, but he was sure that there was a way to get him back. He had seen it in his dreams many times. He would be standing in Nathan's room, ready to fight off whoever it was that was going to try to take him. He had been the equivalent of a superhero, in those dreams.

But there had been something else. Since Nathan's disappearance, Tyler seemed to live in a constant state of déjà vu. He would turn on the radio and narrate entire segments of morning talk shows, answering questions before the hosts could. One of the voices would say "What's the weather looking like for today, Jim?" And Tyler would answer, "Oh, it's going to be a beautiful seventy degrees, not a cloud in the sky, Barb!"

Jinx. Jim owed Tyler a soda.

When a new big story would surface, and

someone at the office would say, "You won't be-lieve what happened!" Tyler would say "School bus went over a bridge, but all the kids made it out okay?" To which they would scoff at him and say, "You heard it on the radio." But he hadn't. None of this made Tyler feel any less crazy, which is why he kept these things to himself.

But the truth was that Tyler wasn't surprised by this new gift—ability—whatever it was. He had seen much stranger things in his lifetime.

8

The first time it occurred to Tyler that he was a little different was when he was twelve years old. The gym teacher, Coach Harris, had an awful habit of starting his class doing something—playing a game, watching a movie—and disappearing. Most likely so he could fuck his favorite thing from the high school, Paula Hodges, in his locked office.

On this particular day, Tyler was on the losing team, as usual. The game was dodge ball. They were told that if Coach Harris wasn't back by the time everyone was out, to start over. Everyone had been out four times now, and it had become ridiculous. The other team was led by a snotty little prick named Chad Myers. Chad and his goons had been playing dirty, aiming for faces. As the fifth game began, Tyler did his best to stay in the game long enough to be the last person to be pummeled. He succeeded. Chad was also the last person left on his team.

"Come on you little bitch!" Chad sneered. "Let's see what you got!"

Tyler reared back with all of his strength and aimed his dodge ball directly at Chad's groin. *I can play dirty, too.*

But he missed, and that was a mistake, because all the balls were literally now in Chad's court.

Tyler just stood there, fuming, feeling defeated. He wasn't the most athletic kid, but he had tried so hard, if for no other reason than to shut the other team up.

"This is gonna hurt, ya little faggot," Chad told him.

Tyler half braced himself, half tried to run from the ball. He awkwardly danced around the gym holding his crotch like he had to pee, some of the kids laughed. As Chad released the ball from his hand as quickly as he could make it go, Tyler dove to his right—sliding across the gym floor and scraping his knee—but he had succeeded in dodging that fucking ball. His friends and teammates cheered for him, but the game wasn't over yet. Tyler scrambled to his feet keeping one eye on Chad as he picked up the ball that had just missed him. Then both of them stood there—each of them holding a ball—

waiting for the other to make his move. Tyler was feeling confident now, he might as well be a pitcher for the Twins as he winded back with his ball. Chad did the same. Both of them let go of their ball at nearly the same time. Tyler's ball whizzed through the air—seemingly in slow motion—and connected with the wall behind Chad's head. But it didn't matter that he had missed, because Chad's ball had connected with Tyler's hands. Tyler had caught the ball, winning the match.

Tyler's friends went crazy, each of them jumping up and down, laughing and cheering. The nerds had won a sports match, no matter how insignificant or stupid it was, they were champions. Tyler was a champion. But then it hit him—literally. In the midst of all the excitement, Chad had picked up one of the balls next to his feet, walked closer to Tyler, and launched it into the side of his face, causing Tyler to fall over and smack his head against the hard gym floor.

Tyler's ears were ringing. Not just the one that had been struck by the ball either. All he could hear was a loud, yet soothing humming. He could feel his body vibrating, time seemed to slow down. He felt unstoppable. He felt like a god. The hairs on his body stood on end, and he smiled. It was a twisted, cynical type of smile. He turned to face Chad and concentrated hard. Suddenly all of the dodge balls in the gym started rising into the air in a startling whoosh. Chad screamed as he turned to run. The first one whacked Chad in the face, knocking him over like his ball had done to Tyler. He tried to back away from Tyler with fear in his eyes, doing a strange, backwards crab walk with his feet and hands. The next ball hit him in the stomach. He cried out in pain and braced for the next blow. After each ball had hit him—which seemed to last forever but actually only lasted about ten seconds—they all fell to the ground, lifeless once again.

It was around this time that Coach Harris returned to the gym to find a room full of students who were in shock. A few of the girls were crying, some of them were screaming, but most of them were just silent, not able to comprehend or believe what they had seen. Chad had been reduced to a wet napkin that had missed the trash can at a frat party—lamely lying in the corner in the fetal position, his eyes wide open.

"What happened here?" Asked Coach Harris.

A few of the students pointed at Tyler, who was

still standing in the same place, smiling the maniacal smile and breathing heavily. Coach Harris walked over to him and looked into his eyes.

"Hello? Roydman? Are you home?" He asked.

Tyler snapped out of it—shaking his head—and instinctively felt the urge to wipe his nose with the back of his hand. His hand came away wet, and a deep red color. His nose was bleeding badly. And there was the smell stuck in his nose—it smelled like a bag full of pennies.

"Jesus, Tyler, you've got a broken nose." Harris said. "And then what, you got revenge?" He added, looking at the wet napkin in the corner.

"I…" Tyler began, "I'm not sure what happened, sir. We were playing, and I won, and then he hit me in the face with a ball. And after that…well, you came in."

"Oh, right. So Myers kicked his own ass?"

"I don't know."

"Course you don't."

Coach Harris walked over to Chad to ask him his side of the story and Tyler's friends all gathered around him.

"Dude! How did you-?"

"How did I what?"

"The balls, they all just kind of flew at him. And you....you were laughing. It was scary," his friend Jeremy told him.

Tyler had no recollection of any of it.

Coach Harris was unsuccessful in getting Chad to tell his side of the story. He was closed for business—come back later.

He sent Tyler to the nurse to have her take a look at his broken nose. But it wasn't broken. It hadn't been hit at all.

Tyler didn't tell his parents the truth about what had happened, he didn't want his mom freaking out; and besides, he didn't even *really* know what had happened anyway. Tyler and Chad both received three days of suspension for fighting. Coach Harris couldn't admit that he wasn't even supervising his class, so he told the principal that they had gotten into a fight in class, and he had broken it up—never mind the class full of students who saw what actually happened. They were just stupid kids, no one would believe them. Luckily for him, nobody did believe them.

Most of the kids started believing that it never really happened, since that's what they had been told repeatedly. Tyler wasn't sure what to think.

Everyone had *told* him what had happened, but if he didn't remember, how could he be sure?

After that day, Chad Myers didn't bully anyone ever again. Something had changed in him when the event which never occurred, occurred.

9

The next time Tyler Roydman did something extraordinary, was when he was fourteen years old. His mom had come home from the store and beeped the horn for Tyler to come and help her bring the groceries inside the house. Tyler came outside, grumbling—the way most teenagers do—and helped his mother. As she went inside with the first few bags, Tyler reached into the trunk of his mother's Buick to grab some bags—when he felt it. His body seemed to vibrate, and he heard a loud humming.

It's happening again, it's real, oh my God, it's happening again.

Tyler turned around and saw what was happening. Their neighbor, Ms. Ethel—who was probably a hundred and fifty years old—was backing her old Lincoln town car out of her driveway, never mind the fifteen-ton school bus that was careening down the road, headed straight for her car. There was about to be a terrible accident, and the school bus was full of children. Tyler dropped the bags he was holding and shouted in the direction of her car. It wasn't any particular word that he shouted at her— more of a sound—something like "Ayhh!!"

But it didn't matter.

Even if she wasn't almost completely deaf, all that could be heard was the screeching of the tires and brakes on the bus, trying their hardest to stop. Somehow he knew that he had to *do* something, but what?

As he ran out into the yard, the rear of the bus began to fishtail to the left, heading straight for his mailbox. Tyler instinctively held his hands up, his right hand in the direction of the bus, his left in the direction of the Lincoln. He felt silly when he thought of doing what he was about to try, but he had to try. He concentrated all of his willpower to *push* the Lincoln—with clueless Ms. Ethel in it and all—back up in the driveway. The car shifted itself from reverse to drive, and lunged forward a whole car length, stopping short of the garage. At the same time, he was using his right hand to correct the way the bus was curving, straightening it out and bringing it to a steady stop.

Tyler the hero.

Tyler's mom returned from putting the bags inside, wondering what was taking him so long to bring the rest inside. She found him collapsed in the driveway, his nose bleeding profusely.

After the incident with the school bus, Tyler realized that there was something definitely different about him. He also realized that what his friends had told him about the dodge ball incident also must have been true. The first time, he had blacked out and didn't remember anything. The next time things were much clearer, and there was no denying that he had used some kind of unknown power to stop a terrible thing from happening. And what Tyler was most certain of, was that in both cases, he was *meant* to do what he did.

The right place at the right time.

10

At the age of nineteen, Tyler had begun to wonder if he would ever have one of his experiences again. He somehow knew that he would, and that when the time came, he would be prepared.

He had taken a writing job for *The Monticello Times* six months prior, and had started dating a girl named Ashleigh. His job was definitely somewhere he could move up with and he felt proud to be able to tell people that he was a writer—or at least he would be after he had put in a little bit of time working on the classified ads.

Everyone's gotta start somewhere.

One cold January night, Tyler was taking Ashleigh out to see a movie at the drive-in theater. It was a monster movie called *Cloverfield*. They took her parent's SUV so that they could turn it backwards and lie down in the back to watch the movie. Tyler wasn't sure if he was more excited to see the movie (it had been produced by J.J. Abrams, the creator of *LOST*) or to have Ashleigh snuggled up next to him under a blanket, horny as hell.

They enjoyed the movie (what they had seen) and enjoyed each other even more. Tyler was absolutely positive that he would marry Ashleigh one day. After the movie, they talked all the way to Ashleigh's parent's house (she was still living at home) about whether or not the camera batteries could have lasted that long, and whether or not something had fallen in the water at the end. Tyler loved that he had found someone with whom he could discuss important matters like whether or not the monster in the movie was hiding under the ocean all along or had come from outer space.

When they got to her parent's house, he walked her to the door and kissed her goodnight; then he drove back to his apartment and found sleep.

He awoke in a panicked state. He glanced at the clock—1:30 AM—his bed seemed to shake—no—vibrate. And there was that loud, yet soothing humming.

Here we go.

He climbed out of his bed and turned on the first light he could find, a lamp on the bedside table. He discovered that his dog Sawyer—a yappy little dachshund—was doing what he did best—yapping. But his yapping wasn't directed at the door, or at the window like it usually was, it was directed at Tyler. He reached out to calm him by patting his head, but Sawyer snapped at his hand and backed away. It was as if he didn't know who he was.

Stranger danger.

Tyler backed away from him, grabbed a handful of clothes from the dresser, and backed out of his bedroom, closing the door in the dog's face. Sawyer told Tyler to get the fuck out, only through the door.

"Stupid little shit!" Tyler yelled at the door.

Tyler got dressed and headed towards the front door of his apartment, grabbing his car keys. He didn't know where he was going, but he knew he was supposed to go somewhere. He opened the door and headed out into the night.

He turned the ignition and the radio came on. Freddie Mercury was expressing his appreciation for fat-bottomed girls. He looked in the rear view mirror to discover that the bottom half of his face was covered in blood.

Of course it was.

He used some napkins—which he was pretty

sure he had already blown his nose into—to wipe his face. He put the car in reverse and headed for the exit of the apartment complex's parking lot. But which way should he turn?

Left, something inside him told him, *Turn left.* He turned left. He followed the road until he came to an intersection, and he had no immediate feeling of what to do next, so he continued on straight for nine more miles until he felt that twinge of intuition rearing its head again.

Turn right here. Then turn off your headlights and follow the wooded path slowly.

He followed the path to the right, with his headlights off, wondering why he couldn't be normal. He couldn't be Patrick Walker, with the baseball scholarship, or Devon Stellmach, with his signed rock band. He was Tyler Roydman, with the bloody noses, and the 1:30 AM crazydrives.

Stop here, said his inner something.

He stopped the car and turned off the ignition. The house at the end of the wooded path was a large brown one with two stories. It was set off the road by a quarter-mile of woods and a dirt trail. The yard was filled with dozens of trees, their branches heavy with snow. He let out a harsh, visible breath in the cold car and opened the door. As soon as he stepped up and out of the car, he heard a muffled scream. He shut the car door quietly and looked around, searching for the source of the scream. It was coming from inside the house. He had parked far enough from the house that his car couldn't be seen through all the trees, and he used them as cover as he approached the house on foot, snow crunching underneath his feet with each step. There were no lights on except for a dim glow from the window on the ground looking into the basement. He worked his way slowly towards the window when he heard another scream come from inside the house, from inside the basement. When he made it to the window, he had to lie on the ground so that he could see inside the house. He shivered when he looked, not because he was cold lying in the damp snow (he was) but because he saw a disturbing scene. There was a girl in her early twenties, kneeling on the floor with her hands tied together above her head in the 12 o'clock position. Long chains came down from the ceiling to hold her hands in place. She was completely naked, and had gashes on her breasts and stomach. Even with the blindfold over her eyes, he could tell that she was a beautiful girl. Her dark hair fell down over one of her shoulders, her skin pale and littered with artistic tattoos. Her head jerked from side to side as she cried for help—and Tyler knew why he was there.

He looked around the room, as far as the small window would let him, and couldn't see anyone else. He inspected the window to see if there was a way to enter the basement without breaking it—he didn't want to be too loud. He pushed gently on the glass, and as he did he heard the sound of snow crunching behind him.

"Nighty night," a man's voice told him as he crashed a two-by-four into the back of his head.

Tyler went nighty night.

11

When he woke, he found that he was in the same position as the young woman he had seen through the window. In fact, he was only a few feet away from her. His hands were tied with chains that hung from the ceiling, only he was sitting instead of kneeling. When he looked down he saw why he was so cold—he was also missing his clothes. He looked over at the girl, she was shivering violently on the cold basement floor, and he noticed that she was still blindfolded.

"You're probably wondering why you ain't got a blindfold, too, am I right?" the voice of the man in the corner of the room said.

Tyler didn't respond.

"No?" he continued, "Well I was debatin' on whether or not I ought to blindfold the girl, too. I mean ain't neither one of ya gonna live to report me or anything like that, ya know?" he tilted his head back and laughed.

Come on, do your thing, Tyler told his inner whatever.

"I'll be honest with you two," the man said, "I been wantin' to do this for a long time now, and now that you're here," he said, looking at Tyler, "I've stumbled across a two-for-one special. I don't know where you come from boy, but I have to imagine it's fate."

The man started across the room and stepped out of the shadows. He was wearing a police officer's uniform. He was an average looking guy, with glasses and a beer belly. He could be a deacon at the church.

He walked over to the girl, leaned over and began smelling her hair. She whimpered.

"Leave her alone," Tyler said.

"You don't like this?" the man asked him as he squeezed both of her breasts firmly, causing her to cry out. "You mean to tell me this doesn't get you *hard*?"

Tyler looked around the room for a weapon of some sort, even though he was chained up. The only one he could find was the pistol in the officer's holster.

Tyler opened his mouth to speak, but the man

cut him off.

"What you don't know is I'm doing the world a favor tonight." He told him. "This bitch right here is the perfect example of why a police officer's job is so hard. I can't tell you how many times we've been called out to her place for a domestic violence dispute, but then when we get there, guess what? She tells us nothing happened. She lets him beat the piss out of her, and then the very next day she's ridin' his cock like it's a goddamned ferris wheel." He scowled in her direction, and Tyler could see that she was crying silently. "So then guess what?" the man continued, "I get a call sayin' there's a couple fightin' at the bar on 5th and Main. I was in the area, so I responded. And there ya go, I coulda put money on who it would be. When I get there I see her sitting there at a table by herself, and I knew it was my chance. I knew that she had to be *punished* for her ignorance. The manager at the bar told me that her boyfriend had drove off with their car, so I offered to give her a ride home—wrapped my jacket around her and all—it was a real show. Only we didn't go to her house. You see, police officers are here to *help,* and if you ignore that help, then you ought to be made into an example. And in a few days, when I discover her body in the snow with her boyfriend's DNA all over it, people will say 'oh poor thing, she should have reported him instead of letting him run all over her like she did.' And I'll be a hero for putting him away."

Tyler could see that the officer was proud of himself. He had thought everything through.

"And where do I fit into this scenario?" Tyler asked him.

"Well I can't just give you ALL my secrets now can I? It's so much more fun if it's a *surprise*!"

The officer got close enough to him that Tyler could smell the tuna sandwich he had eaten for dinner. Tyler looked at his badge which said that his name was Officer Mills.

Tyler tried to make something happen with his mind the way he had done two times before, but he wasn't having any luck. The girl cried out next to him for the officer to please let her go, that she wouldn't say anything.

Fuck that, Tyler thought. That wasn't his style.

"Please Officer, please! I'm innocent. It wasn't me sir!" Officer Mills shouted and added, "You need to shut your mouth, whore, if you know what's good for you."

"Look at me," Tyler said to him. He had an idea.

Officer Mills looked at Tyler.

"I'm going to kill you tonight." Tyler told him.

Officer Mills snorted as if he had just heard a good joke. If he had been eating cereal, milk would be coming out of his nose.

"Not if I kill *you* first," he said with a laugh.

"You couldn't kill anything. You don't have the balls." Tyler said. He could *feel* the nameless girl next to him thinking *shut the fuck up!*

Mills swooped down like an eagle attacking a rodent so he could get eye level with Tyler.

"I don't have the balls?"

"That's what I said."

Mills slowly reached down and grabbed Tyler's scrotum, squeezing hard. Tyler howled in pain.

"Well maybe I can have some of yours! What do you think? You seem to have plenty!" He shouted, spit flying in Tyler's face.

Tyler had never felt such terrible pain. It was as if a grizzly bear was trying to claw its way out of his abdomen. Without any warning, he vomited down the front of Officer Mill's uniform.

"You nasty son-of-a-bitch!" Mills yelled out.

But Tyler barely heard what he said. Instead he heard a loud humming.

Bingo.

"Ya know what?" Mills said, "I'm done playing games with you." He drew his pistol from its holster. "And I was gonna let you watch, too." He said as he pointed it at Tyler's face.

But Tyler was already in control.

His nose was bleeding badly which didn't bother Tyler at all, it was a good thing.

Officer Mills had a look of horror on his face as he involuntarily raised his gun away from Tyler's face and pointed it at the chains that held him in place. His hands were trembling in a battle for free will. Finally, with extreme concentration on Tyler's part, the gun shot the chains that held him in place, freeing him, and causing the girl to jump and yelp. The gunshots were nearly deafening in the vast, concrete basement. What happened next was unplanned however. Officer Mills had managed to break free of Tyler's mind's grasp and aimed the gun back at his face, and smiled as he pulled the trigger.

This is it. I can't believe it ends like this.

Only Tyler wasn't dead, because a bullet never

struck him. Because *somehow* the bullet never left the gun, causing the gun to explode violently sending a piece of metal into Officer Mill's throat. Blood spilled out of the hole in his throat and he fell down on the ground making choking sounds. Tyler searched him to see if he had any more weapons, and he found a large knife in his pocket. Tyler wasn't concerned with finishing him off. Mills was too busy holding both hands to his throat and painting his basement floor a new shade of red.

Tyler began working on freeing the girl. He pulled the blindfold off of her eyes and told her that it was going to be okay. She was in shock, but she shook her head that she understood. He used the knife that he had taken from Mills and cut her hands free of the leather straps attached to the chains. He helped her to stand up, and she hugged him. She had tears in her eyes. After making sure that Mills was dead, they walked up the stairs and into the house. They searched for their clothes but were unable to find them. Tyler figured they had been burned or buried already. They found some blankets in a closet and covered themselves up, partly because of shame, mostly because of hypo-thermia. As they sat on the couch Tyler began to wonder if she would ever speak. Finally she did, barely audible.

"What's your name?"

"Tyler, and yours?"

"Laura... Laura Leigh."

They sat quietly for a moment longer on the couch. Finally, Tyler stood up and said that he was going to look for a phone. He walked into the kitchen and searched all of the counters—no luck. He returned with a bottle of water for Laura. She thanked him, and he nodded towards the door behind her, as if to say *I'm going to check in there now*.

He entered the room and immediately recognized it as Mill's bedroom. A queen size bed was in the middle of the room, the closet door hung open with multiple police uniforms hanging in it. He found a phone plugged in next to the bed. He reached down and picked it up. When he turned around to exit the bedroom, his foot hit something, a large notebook with loose pages jutting out of the sides. He walked out of the bedroom and called the police as he thumbed through the notebook. It was filled with the list of girls Mills had planned to kidnap, and with detailed instructions on how he would get away with it.

45

Tyler thumbed through the notebook in horror. There were over twenty names of potential victims. Starting with Laura Leigh Adkins.

When the police arrived, Laura told them how Tyler had rescued her, how she was already dead, and he had seemingly come from nowhere and saved her life. The officers discovered their coworker, Mills, in the basement.

"Jesus Christ." one of the young officers said. "It's a fucking mess, sir."

Sir was a detective by the name of Dugger.

Detective Dugger walked down the stairs into the basement, and after just a few moments he returned with a question.

"Who killed him?" he asked, looking at Tyler.

"I already gave my statement, sir." Tyler responded.

"Did I ask you if you had given a statement? I said who fucking killed him?"

"His gun exploded when he tried to shoot me."

"Exploded? Guns don't just explode. I need the truth."

Another officer interrupted.

"The gun is down there, sir. It's in a million pieces."

Dugger shot the officer a look that said *I didn't ask you a goddamn thing.*

"It's true," Tyler started, "he shot my chains, and then he tried to shoot me, but it just exploded."

"What I need to know," Dugger said, "is *why* you came here."

Tyler looked away for a second in thought before he answered.

"To save her." He said, gesturing towards Laura.

"But how did you *know* about her predicament? Unless of course, you were in on it?"

Tyler stared at Dugger in disbelief.

"I have never met either of these people in my life. I woke up and felt the *need* to come here.. I just.. somehow knew where to go. I can't explain it." Tyler said.

Tyler didn't tell the officers about his past—about the dodgeball incident, or the bus. He wondered if he should, but even now, they already thought he was crazy, he figured it wouldn't help.

"So you're a psychic then? Look everybody! We got a psychic superhero over here!" Dugger said, his expression blank.

Another officer approached Dugger holding the

notebook that Tyler had found under the bed. He said something to him in a low voice. Dugger took the notebook, turned away from Tyler, and stepped outside with it. The notebook would never be seen by anyone again.

Tyler did not like Dugger at all. There was something unsettling about a man of his temperament having so much power. And as it turned out, Dugger shared the dislike for Tyler. Most men would consider him a hero. But Tyler wasn't a hero. He was the person who uncovered a corrupt officer in his department. And he wouldn't forget it.

12

The community was divided. There were many who praised Tyler for being in the right place at the right time. But there were skeptics who had to ask things like: what was he doing driving up to a stranger's house so far from his own at 2:00 AM? And were they maybe working together?

Some people couldn't let a good thing be a good thing.

Of course, Ashleigh wanted answers to these questions as well. Tyler finally broke down and told her everything. About his nosebleeds, about the bus, and the dodgeball game. She nodded as he told her, not in an understanding way, but in an *I'm not deaf* kind of way. When he finally finished talking, she thought for a moment before speaking.

"So you can.. like.. you just *know* when something bad will happen?"

"Not always.. It's only happened a few times. And when it does, I don't ever really know what I'm going to do, it just happens."

"That's insane."

"You don't believe me."

"No, it's not that I don't believe you.. I just don't know how to feel about it. I mean, have you ever told anyone else?"

"No."

"Why not?"

Tyler paused, and thought hard.

"Well, because it scares the hell out of me. I mean would you tell anyone?"

"I would have told you." She said.

His face turned red.

"What should I have said? 'Hi, I'm Tyler and I'm pretty sure I have some kind of superpowers?'"

"You don't have to be a dick."

After some time, they discussed it less frequently, until it was just a thing in the back of their minds—like an old phone number, useless information.

They were married just two years later, and Nathan was born two years after that.

13

After Nathan went missing, Anne Weaver was in charge of writing the articles about the occurrence. She would smile when she saw Tyler in the hallway, and then she would bash him in the papers. When Tyler went to his boss, Mr. Sanderfer, to tell him that he didn't appreciate what she was doing, Mr. Sanderfer would act appalled at her actions, but nothing had been done about it. Tyler knew the truth though, they all wanted him gone. Whether he had committed a crime or not, he was a bad splotch on the image of the paper. They couldn't fire him— there would be a massive lawsuit for sure—but they *could* try to get him to quit. And it didn't hurt that their papers sold four times as many copies when stories about the Roydman kid were on the front page.

Originally, Tyler did want to quit. He had ap-plied at other places, but for *some* reason he didn't receive any calls for interviews. And after a while, when he realized he was seemingly stuck, he started to take pleasure in showing up to work every day, just to see the looks on their faces.

He's still here.

He was lonely, and felt singled out. With him still being separated from his wife, he didn't know who to turn to, so he wrote stories to escape reality.

He had written several, but he never got any published. He was somewhat of a star among some nerdy writers on an online writing forum. He also found that this was an excellent way to talk about what had happened in his life without *really* talking about it. His most popular story was *Erase Traces*. The story loosely told of his run in with a particularly corrupt officer of the law. He wrote under a pseudonym, it made him feel more at ease about discussing such sensitive topics.

Now, Tyler was settling in after work on that rainy April day in which he had locked his keys in his car. He figured he should have known he would and avoided it—with the déjà vu and all—but hey, one can't be perfect all the time.

"You're losing your touch," he said to the mirror above his computer desk.

More like losing my mind, he thought.

He opened his laptop and stared at the desktop for several seconds before opening the Internet browser. The wallpaper was a photo of Nathan running around the front yard with a sparkler in his hand. He couldn't believe it had been almost three years since that day.

He sighed and reached for his pipe. He had read in a book once that in order to truly get over a loss of a loved one, you need to attack your problems stone sober. Tyler figured that advice was probably great for someone who was actually trying to get over someone, but he hadn't given up yet. He never would. And besides, the weed helped him write.

He logged on to the writers' forums he frequented, where he talked with the people he considered his friends (or the closest thing possible, considering he didn't even use a real name). When he had signed in to his account he saw that he had received three messages. Two of them were from other writers he had been talking to, but the third was from someone whose screen name he didn't recognize. He opened the first email and scanned over it quickly. It was another writer asking when his next story was going to be finished. The second email was more of the same. Then he clicked on the link to open the third email. There was no subject, and it only contained one sentence: *They found you, be in touch.*

He stared at the screen for several minutes with a blank expression on his face. Who found him? Who would be in touch? He thought it was probably a joke or a mistake, but at the same time, he *knew* that this was coming eventually. He didn't know how he knew or even what it meant, but he knew that *they* meant trouble for him.

He spent a great deal of his evening thinking about the message. There was an ominous feeling in his core, something telling him that his life was about to change. And later that evening, as he laid down to go to sleep, he embraced the humming, and the vibrating bed, and damn if he wasn't going to ruin his pillowcase.

14

As he was sleeping, he entered a lucid dream state. He was aware of what was happening to him as if he wasn't asleep. It felt as if he had unlocked a piece of his consciousness he had known was there but could never access. He opened his eyes and found himself in a long, winding hallway with thousands of doors. He walked forward a few steps and noticed that his feet weren't making any noise. He looked down and felt his stomach flutter—the way it would when he missed a step on a staircase—and he tried to scream, but his mouth wouldn't utter a sound. He was seemingly floating on nothing. When he looked up, he noticed that the ceiling was nothing more than swirling, cloudy blackness. He ran down the hallway to see how far it went. After realizing that he wasn't getting anywhere, he stopped and decided to open a door. All of the doors were tall wooden ones with great ornate silver fixtures placed on them. It was as if each of them led into a luxurious mansion. He grabbed the handle of the door closest to him on his right and turned it. He hesitated for a moment but finally he opened the door. When he stepped through it, he found himself in a room which was completely white. The floor, the walls, everything in the room was a radiant, blinding white. There was something else. As soon as he entered the room, he noticed that the solidness of the floor returned, and the air seemed to hold the weight that it should. He tried to speak.

"H-hello?" He said to the room.

Please, take a seat, an ominous, booming voice said as a massive white table appeared in the middle of the room, at the end of it there was a single white chair.

He walked slowly to the chair and placed a hand on it, marveling over the make of it. It was unlike anything he had ever seen; it was almost...*alien.* He thought about how crazy it was that he was following the instructions of a faceless voice in an empty room, but then again, there weren't many things that shocked him. He sat down in the chair and waited for something to happen. Finally the voice spoke again, thundering throughout the room.

We are pleased that you have found your way to us, Mr. Roydman.

Tyler straightened up in the chair, feeling uneasy and unsure what to say.

"Who is *we*?" He said finally, looking around the room in frustration.

We are who you want us to be.

Tyler wondered what they meant by that.

"I don't know what that means."

We will make this easier for you to understand. We are the ones who put this all here. We are the ones who brought life to your planet. We are your creators.

He thought about the last word that the voice had said.

Creators.

Something about the way that was said sent a chill down his spine.

"So you're saying you're God." Tyler stated.

The voice uttered a harsh, flat laugh which echoed off the walls like a renegade racquetball.

God, Satan, whoever you want us to be.

Tyler wasn't an overly religious person, he had always found it hard to fully commit to Christianity—he saw too many flaws which were hard to ignore—but he felt uneasy hearing a voice tell him that he was God *or* Satan.

"How do I know that this isn't just a crazy dream I'm having? I mean...I went to sleep, and now I'm here suddenly."

But you do know, don't you? That this is real? You've known for some time we think. After all, you are a Variant. One of the strongest minded ones we have ever encountered. It would be hard to believe you didn't know.

Tyler's head was spinning. He *did* know he wasn't dreaming, even if he found it hard to admit. His heart was thrashing in his chest, and he was emitting a cold sweat. What was that word they used? *Variant?*

"Variant?" he said, his voice creaking.

Yes. You have discovered your abilities; do you not know what they are for?

"I don't know what you're talking about." Tyler lied.

Oh come now, do not lie to us, Tyler. We do not like being lied to.

"Why am I here?" he asked, "I mean what do you want from me?"

There was a pause which seemed to go on forever. The room felt cold and uncomfortable.

We need you to fix your mistake.

15

Tyler opened his eyes and found himself in his room, drenched in sweat. His head ached, and he felt like he was going to be sick. He got out of bed and ran to the bathroom, kneeling at the toilet like an underage girl at a frat party.

"What the fuck?" he said to the toilet, his voice strained.

The toilet didn't respond.

After the queasy feeling passed, he left the bathroom and headed for the kitchen. He found the aspirin bottle in the medicine cabinet and took two pills with a bottle of water. He sat down at the table with his water and looked at the clock on the wall. It was only 10:30. He had only slept for a few minutes. It had felt like hours, days even. He got up from the table and walked outside, looking up at the sky. He thought of all of the implications that this new discovery had brought. He was tired of feeling like he might have been crazy and decided to just embrace it. He figured if he was out of his mind that it was already too late for him, and besides, pretending what he was seeing wasn't real wasn't going to help anyone because it was still happening to him. Maybe if these *Creators* needed him to fix something, that was really what it meant; it didn't *have* to be a bad thing. But what did they need from him? What was his mistake that he needed to fix? As far as he knew, he had done everything that he was supposed to in those instances when he had a...calling to do so. It was also hard to ignore the other thing that the voice had said.

We are who you want us to be.

He wondered if this was less inviting than it sounded.

We can be your worst nightmare if you don't do as we say, is what it seemed they had meant.

And why would they need *him* to do anything for them? If they really were the Creators of the world, couldn't they just do anything they wanted to? Maybe they just enjoyed messing with people. Isn't that what a child does with ants in the dirt? But then there was that word they had used. They had called him a *Variant*. So did that mean there were others out there like him? They wouldn't have a word for it unless there was a whole group of them. He walked out into the yard and opened his car door. Reaching inside, he felt under the seat and grabbed a pack of Camel menthols. He had no one to hide them from, except himself. He had decided that he was done smoking, but he had saved this pack for emergencies—and it was an emergency. He opened the pack and inhaled the minty, earthy scent. Cigarettes always smelled better before they were lit. With a slight twinge of guilt, and a stronger twinge of excitement, he lit the cigarette and breathed in. He had only gotten serious about smoking after Nathan had gone missing. He didn't know why he quit either. Right now it was seeming to be a terrible idea. His head was buzzing and he walked back to the porch and sat down in a chair. He decided that he needed to find out as much as he could about Variants. And somehow he had to fix something that he didn't know he had broken.

The next morning Tyler was sitting at his desk at work wondering why he even showed up. It wasn't that he didn't need the money, it was just that the creators of the fucking universe had given him an order. But he didn't know what to do. He tried searching the internet but he wasn't able to find anything on Variants. And he was positive that he still didn't know what mistake needed fixing. When it came time for lunch, he stood up from his desk and headed towards the door. Jimmy seemed to form out of thin air in front of Tyler as he was about to exit the building.

"Hey champ! Where you headed for lunch?" Jimmy asked him.

"Oh...uh well I had promised my mom I would take her out today, I haven't taken her out to lunch in forever. And you know...moms," Tyler said with an awkward, short laugh.

"Oh, yeah that's cool man. I was thinking of going to my grandma's place and baking her some cookies." Jimmy said with a wink, before walking away laughing.

Tyler felt bad lying to Jimmy, he was the only one in the office who he could really stand to be around for more than five minutes, and he had blown him off too many times before. But today he really felt he needed to go to the library. He walked outside and inhaled the cool, Minnesota air. He was a fan of the weather in his state, snow and all. He had gone to Florida once with his family, and he swore he would never come back. The heat and the humidity was just too much.

He got in his car and before he even cranked it, he knew that Jim James would be singing about evil urges. He turned the key and there he was:

Evil urges baby; they're part of the human way.
It ain't evil baby; if ya ain't hurting anybody.

He suddenly had a thought that he was surprised he hadn't had before.

Why didn't he know about the Creators before he met them?

He knew small things, like what song would be on the radio, or what someone would do or say. But some things felt foreign. The déjà vu only worked some of the time. He wondered how it tied in with his other abilities.

Who cares what's going to be on the radio next, he thought, *how about some fucking insight on something that matters?*

He left the parking lot and drove down to the town library. When he arrived, there were only two other cars in the parking lot. It wasn't a busy place. He got out and admired the building. It held a strong sense of nostalgia for him. He liked coming here when he was young. His parents would take him several times a week at his request. He thought it might have had an influence on his decision to become a writer, the way that the library made him feel warm and happy, being around all those books.

He got out of his car and walked inside the building. The lady who worked behind the counter, her name was Gloria. Gloria had worked at the library since they first opened their doors a million years ago, and she knew everything about everything. As usual, when Tyler passed her she smiled the fake smile that she always did, the one that said *You ought to be in jail for what you done.* But Tyler didn't concern himself with her opinion of him, the way a cat could give a shit less whether you came home or not, as long as you fed them. He ignored her and went into the nonfiction section. For a long time he just stood in one place staring at the books. He had no idea what to look for or why he thought he would when he got there. Maybe his subconscious just wanted him to be in a comfortable place, even if Gloria *was* flashing him the stink-eye. But no, there had to be *something* here.

Without any reason behind it, he started pulling books out at random and searching through them.

He looked at dozens of books, from all different sections, searching for nothing in particular. After some time, he looked down at his watch and realized that he was already late for returning to work. He put the books he was holding back on the shelf and walked away towards the exit, feeling disappointed. He was sure that he was supposed to come here. But for what?

As he was pushing the door open to leave the library, he felt a vibration in his bones, and Gloria was telling him to have a good day with a fake smile. But Tyler didn't hear "have a good day," he heard a loud humming. He held one hand to his nose, stopping the blood from coming out before it could start, and with his other hand he held up a finger which was universal for *hold on lady, I'm not leaving yet.* He turned left down from the front desk and made his way into the men's room. Once inside, he grabbed a handful of paper towels, ran them under the water to wet them, and wiped his face. He left the faucet on so he could wash his hands. He managed to avoid looking in the mirror—it was something he always did; he wasn't comfortable looking into his own eyes. After he washed his hands, he left the bathroom and headed back into the library. As if he was being pulled by an invisible string, he walked right up to a shelf in the back of the library. The whole section was covered in dust; it seemed it was just a nameless section of old books no one would ever want to read—the kind that all looked like old encyclopedias from ages ago, real doorstoppers. But then he noticed something. One of the panels didn't match the rest. It was discolored like it had been replaced. He looked around to see if anyone was watching—the way people did before they started talking about someone—and confirmed that he was alone. He felt for the edge of the paneling and picked at it with his fingertips. Once he had a good hold of it, he pulled hard, jarring it out of place. There was a small blue book standing up inside the hole he had made. He picked it up and read the cover aloud: *The Man in The Mirror.*

He opened the book and thumbed through its pages. It appeared to be an old book—it was covered in dust. It had been here for a long time. He turned the book over to look at the spine. He only found one word. It was in the place where you would find the author's name. His hands were shaking as he read it. He hastily replaced the panel he had removed and tucked the book inside his jacket. After he left the library, he couldn't stop thinking about the word he found on the spine.

ROYDMAN.

16

When Tyler got home from work, he set his bag down on the couch and pulled the book out of the front pocket. It felt like something he needed to keep hidden, like it was very important. He sat down in his recliner and opened the book, turning to the first page.

CHAPTER ONE

This book contains useful information when found in the right hands. I trust that you already know whether or not it is something which will be beneficial to you. There are many things in which I can attempt to help you with, but a large majority of what I will tell you will be only stepping stones to help you find the information you need. If this book found its way into the wrong hands it could be used against you, so guard it with your life. Now, read with a keen eye, and we may begin.

Just then, Tyler's phone rang. He didn't recognize the number.

"Hello?" Tyler answered.

There was a long pause on the other end of the receiver.

"Hello?" Tyler said again, this time sounding frustrated.

"You found the book already?" The voice said.

"Who is this?"

"Look, I don't have much time, and this is a major risk calling you, but you need to know that they know you found the book. They will not allow you to—"

The line went dead.

Tyler looked down at his phone. The number was a 334 area code. He pulled up the internet browser on his phone and found that the area code belonged to the southeastern part of Alabama. He didn't know anyone from there. He dialed the number back, but it went straight to voicemail.

Tyler's heart was racing. He felt cold sweat creeping out of his pores like tiny ants crawling all over his body. The person who had called him was panicked. Somehow he knew that it was the same person who had sent him the email before. What the hell were these *Creators* up to? He had to find them again, to talk to them. He went to his car, getting another menthol cigarette from under the seat, and paced the front yard in thought. Last time he faced them, he had went to sleep, but maybe he could *will* himself there. He glanced around the yard, feeling as if someone was watching him. He couldn't see anyone, but that didn't ease his mind any. He went back inside and sat on the couch. He pictured the place he wanted to go to in his mind. The long winding hallway with thousands of doors. His hands made fists, and his body started shaking. He could hear the world around him whooshing and humming as he left his world and entered theirs.

Exit stage left.

To his surprise, he quickly found himself in that long, winding hallway with the grand, ornate doors. He didn't know what he meant to do here, but he wanted answers—some kind of explanation for everything that was going on. He walked down the hall, looking for the door he had found last time, when he met the Creators. But all of the doors looked too similar to tell apart. He opened one of the doors at random and saw his mother sitting on her bed, crying. He noticed that she was much younger than she was now. His father walked into the room, he also appeared much younger.

Neither one of them seemed to notice him standing there in the room with them.

"What's wrong?" His father asked her.

She looked up at him, mascara bleeding from her eyes. "It's Tyler." She said before letting out another sob.

"What happened?" His father asked, rushing from the room. Tyler followed him. His father opened the door to his room to find a young Tyler—maybe five years old—asleep in his bed.

"No, he's okay," his mother said from behind them. "It's just that he had one of his episodes today. While you were off doing *whatever.*"

"You mean working?" He whisper-shouted.

"Right. I'm *sure* you're working all these long hours that you say you are. Where is the fucking money to show for it?"

Tyler could tell by his father's expression that he wanted to scream, to punch a wall, anything to get his frustration out. Instead, he calmly asked a question.

"What happened this time?" Each word came

out slower than the last, a sign of impatience.

"Well," she began, "we were at the library."

"You don't say."

"*And*," she continued, "I was sitting there reading *Salem's Lot*, and Tyler was off looking at books about dinosaurs or something, I mean, I was watching him. But then I look up and he's *gone*. And so I walked around the whole library looking for him, and finally I found him back there in the back talking to some creepy old man."

Tyler's skin crawled. He vaguely remembered this.

"What did you do?" His father asked.

"I told him to come to me, and the man was just staring at me like he wanted to talk to me, it was weird. He never spoke, just *stared*. But then the man walked away and Tyler just stood there, twitching. And his nose was bleeding, ruined his favorite shirt."

"Well is he alright now?"

"Well yeah."

"What did he say about the man? Maybe he worked there? I mean isn't that book you're reading about vampires? Maybe you're just being paranoid."

"I said, 'honey who was that man you were talking to?' And he looked at me and said '*what man, mommy?*'"

Tyler noticed his father's worried expression. He had seen that look many times.

"We can take him back to the doctor." He said. "But you know they're gonna want to take him for all kinds of medical tests."

"Maybe that's what he needs." Tyler's mother said.

Suddenly, Tyler was sucked out of the door he entered—as if being pulled backwards by a giant, invisible hand—leaving his parents' old house and landing in the hallway. The door slammed in his face.

They knew. They knew he was different. How did he not know they knew?

He continued walking down the corridor and picked another door at random. It didn't seem to matter anyway. He felt of the doorknob and wrapped his hand around it. Sighing, he prepared himself for what might be inside. He opened the door slowly, peeking inside. It was a normal looking bedroom. There was a closet, photographs hanging on the walls of children smiling, a dresser with a television set on it, and a bed in the middle of the room. Sitting on the bed, turned away from him, was an old man looking out the window. His hair grayed, his skin wrinkled. Tyler gasped when he saw him. He hadn't noticed him at first, when he was admiring the room. But then something unexpected happened. The old man turned his head over his shoulder, as if in reaction to the gasp.

He can hear me? My parents couldn't hear me.

Tyler felt something on his shoulder, which sent a rigid chill down his spine. He looked over and saw a hand on his shoulder, but it wasn't an ordinary hand, it was large, with five long, black fingers. Each fingernail was several inches long and sharp as a razor. Tyler screamed in horror, and the old man on the bed turned around and looked him in the eyes. Just as their eyes met, the old man disappeared into nothing as Tyler exited the room against his will and found himself in the corridor once again. He put his hand on his shoulder and spun in a circle, making sure nothing was behind him.

What IS this place?

"I'm done playing games!" He yelled in the empty hallway. "Show yourselves!"

Down the hall, one of the doors started to illuminate, it was as if the universe was saying *over here you impatient fuck!*

He walked to the door and swung it open. He was not surprised to see that he was in the white room again. He walked to the middle of the room and shouted, "I'm here! What do you want from me?"

He heard a rattling laughter coming from every direction.

We are not swayed by your tenacity, Mr. Roydman, however impressive it may be. You still have not fixed your mistake.

"What mistake?" Tyler bellowed, "and how do I fix it?"

That is for you to find out. This is the problem with our particular structure we have here. You Variants are always causing trouble, and we cannot fix the problem for you.

"Cannot or will not?" He asked.

Please do not misunderstand us. We are not proud of our...need for your help, but it is the only way.

Tyler thought about what they had said. It didn't make sense. If they were the creators of the universe, why would they need anything from him?

"And what happens if I don't figure it out?"

Oh, you will...they always do. But sometimes not without

a little motivation. Maybe you need more time to think and less time to meddle with things you have no business meddling with.

PART TWO
We're Not So Different, You and I

1

Ashleigh Sanders (*not* Roydman, hadn't been Roydman for some time) rolled over in her bed to turn off her alarm clock. It was six in the morning, her usual time to wake up and get ready for work. She had moved into a one-bedroom apartment close to her work downtown. She had furnished it the way she liked, with paintings of lighthouses and with matching furniture. It was small, but she felt comfortable there.

She got up and walked into the kitchen and started a pot of coffee. Her eyes wandered to the fridge, where she had placed several photos. There were plenty of Nathan, a couple of him, Tyler and herself, and one of her with her dad. Even though it made her sad, she loved looking at all of the pictures.

"Miss you guys," she said to the photos.

While the coffee was brewing, she walked down the hall to the bathroom and started the shower. As she undressed, she couldn't help but glance at her legs, with the horizontal scars of several past mistakes. She didn't know if she had ever truly wanted to die, but she hadn't told anyone either, so she wasn't sure why she did it. Most girls would cut themselves for attention. In those moments when she had been so low that it seemed like a good idea to run a razor across her skin, she always wanted to talk to Tyler, but it was so much easier to blame him for what had gone wrong. In truth, it was almost easy to *hate* him.

After she finished showering, she ran a straightener through her hair, put on a nice pair of dark pants and a red blouse, and returned to the kitchen. She poured her coffee and stepped outside to enjoy the cool morning air. Some of the kids who lived in the apartment complex stood at the end of the road by the stop sign, waiting for the bus.

Nathan would be going to kindergarten this year, she thought.

She noticed that her paper had been delivered, it was sitting in the grass in front of her door. One of her habits which she was less than proud of, was that she enjoyed reading the section of the paper that Tyler wrote. Even if it was other people's words, it made her feel close to him—maybe she didn't hate him after all. She brought the paper inside and opened it up as she sat down at the kitchen table. She turned to the classifieds section and began reading. She almost choked on her coffee.

2

Tyler's phone rang. He woke up and looked around, dazed. He was lying in an awkward position—still on the couch—and it was morning. He looked at his phone. It was Ashleigh calling him.

"Hello?" He said, sounding surprised.

"Did you do it?" She asked him.

"Did I do what?"

"Tyler, don't fuck with me! This is serious!"

"I honestly don't know what you're talking about!"

"If you really don't know, then have a look at your newspaper, the classifieds."

"Okay…" He said, walking outside. "What's going to be in there that I don't know about?"

"Exactly," she said.

He grabbed his paper from the ground. Sirens were echoing from a distance.

"Are those sirens?"

"Yeah."

"Jesus Christ."

"*What?*" he said, opening his paper.

But he didn't need an answer. It was right there in black and white. It took up the whole top section of the classifieds. He read his section of the paper in complete, bewildered horror.

My name is Tyler Roydman.

I have worked for this newspaper for ten years with nothing to show for it. Nobody appreciates me, and everyone thinks I killed my own son.

Anne Weaver marched in here like she owned the place and started spewing bullshit about me and my family. I tried to deal with it in a civil manner, but she just kept giving me these nasty looks in the hallway and continued on doing what she was doing. I wanted to hurt her so badly. She also took the job I was meant to have. I finally made up my mind that if I can't make it as a real writer, then I would find another way to become famous. The world will know me now, because I gave that bitch what she deserved: I slit her throat with a pocket knife. It was everything I thought it would be and more. I feel no remorse. I'm not sorry, but I'll bet Anne Weaver is sorry. She said so before I did it, thinking it would save her.

Tyler

"Hello?" Came Ashleigh's voice through the phone.

The sirens were much louder now.

"Ashleigh, I didn't…" He began, "Listen, if I call you, please don't ignore my calls. I… I might need your help."

The police pulled into his yard. First one car, then two, then four. All of the officers got out with their guns drawn.

Tyler put his hands up, dropping the phone onto the ground.

3

Ashleigh sat down, tucked her knees into her chest, and began to cry. She didn't know whether to believe Tyler or not, but it had seemed like he was telling the truth. It didn't seem like him to kill anyone, especially for the reasons he had supposedly listed. And why would he put all of that in the paper? And had they even found a body yet? All of it was almost too much for her to bear. She turned on the television and searched the channels for any news on the incident. She found one—a local station. The anchor was saying how it wasn't surprising considering the fact that he had already gotten away with killing his own son, adding that there had been a new discovery and they would be back after a quick commercial break.

The fucking nerve of these people.

She straightened herself in her chair and waited for the commercials to end. Finally, the broadcast returned and an excited young anchor had some news to give.

This just in: police have found a body inside a residence on 122 Coffman Street. After a typed confession from a local newspaper writer was published earlier this morning, a neighbor went to check on Miss Weaver and called the police when she wouldn't answer the door.

Police entered the home, and found the body of a woman in her bedroom, with her throat slit. This gruesome discovery is of course a terrible tragedy. And although the body is believed to be Miss Weaver herself, police have not confirmed.

There is a suspect in custody.

A mug shot appeared of Tyler's face from years ago, when Nathan disappeared.

Tyler Roydman, a twenty-eight year-old newspaper writer from right here in Monticello, has written his typed confession in the classifieds section of the local newspaper he writes for. This isn't Roydman's first run-in with legal trouble. He was suspected in a kidnapping and attempted rape case when he was nineteen years old, and he was a suspect again, three years ago when his two year old son went missing. In both cases, he was never found guilty. We will keep you updated as more develops.

After the broadcast was over, Ashleigh sat in silence for a long time. Finally, she spoke aloud to the empty room.

"What is going on, Tyler?!"

4

Tyler went quietly with the officers. He knew that there was no fighting what was happening. The Creators had warned him. He was getting time to think about what needed fixing, and punished for meddling.

Meddling with what?

Either way, he didn't see how he could be of any help to anyone if he was stuck behind iron bars. Or dead. He had heard of plenty of people being killed in prison for no good reason.

As he sat in the back of the police cruiser, wondering what coming events would transpire, he began to feel like he'd been there before. There was a smell, like tobacco mixed with the white Valentine's day candy hearts. The ones that had little messages like:

'B MINE' or 'U R FUCKED TYLER'

When the officer picked up an empty water bottle from his middle console, Tyler watched him spit his dip into it. That was that smell, wintergreen snuff. And without even looking at the can in the passenger seat, Tyler knew it was Copenhagen.

When they arrived at the jail, Tyler was finger-printed, stripped, redressed in prison orange, and photographed. His phone had been taken, along with his wallet, and the small amount of change in his pocket. The officers took him down to his cell and ushered him inside, slamming the door behind him.

"Sick fuck," one of them said as he walked away.

Tyler wondered when he could have his phone call. In movies they would always say things like "Hey! I know I get a phone call!" He hoped that was true.

His cell was a small one, with a twin-sized bed which looked about as comfortable as dinner with your sister's new boyfriend. It also had a toilet, just inches away from the bed. It was a steel, cold look-ing thing. There was no mirror, no sink, nothing else, just a bed and a pot. Tyler didn't know which one to sit on first, he hadn't gone to the bathroom in almost twenty-four hours.

Eventually, after several hours, someone came

to tell him it was time for his phone call.

It *was* true.

He figured most people would call a lawyer, or at least a family member who would call a lawyer for them. But Tyler needed to call Ashleigh.

When he picked up the phone and dialed her number, he thought that maybe she wouldn't answer. Maybe this was the final nail in the coffin.

I can deal with a lot of things, Tyler, but this...this is just too much.

But she did answer.

"Hello?" She said, not sure if it was Tyler or not.

"Ashleigh," Tyler began, "Ashleigh listen, there's a book at my house, I *need* it."

He knew the calls were recorded and didn't want to say any more than necessary.

Ashleigh knew that whatever he was asking, it had to be for a reason.

"A book," she said, "Okay, what does it look like?"

"It's small, blue, looks old. Please get it as quick as you can and bring it to me...you know how I am about my books, can't just stop in the middle of a story. I gotta know what happens."

"Okay Tyler, I'll get your book. When is visitation?"

"On Sunday. One o'clock. I already put you on the list. I gotta go, thank you."

"I'll see you Sunday," she said through tears.

After their phone call, Tyler felt hopeful. He knew that there was information from the book that he needed. He wasn't sure what to do next.

That night, when he went to sleep, he woke in the winding hallway again. He was glad; he thought maybe he could find out more about what to do next. He opened a door to his left and he found that he was in the library, and sitting down in front of him, his mother was reading a book. He spoke, to see if she could hear him. She couldn't. He walked around so that he could see the front of the book. It was *Salem's Lot*. Tyler froze. He turned around and saw a five-year-old version of himself, reading a book about dinosaurs. He then walked around to the back side of the library, and there stood the old man his mother had mentioned. He was facing away from Tyler, messing with a bookshelf. He watched him place a book inside, and replace the paneling.

The book.

Tyler walked back around to the other side, and saw that the young version of himself had started walking towards the old man. The man bent down and whispered something in young Tyler's ear, pointing to the bookshelf. By this time, Tyler's mother was frantic, looking for him. She walked right past him, not noticing him standing there, and went to scold young Tyler for disappearing. Tyler followed her. When the old man looked up, Tyler was standing right behind his mother's shoulder watching the exchange. And the old man *saw* Tyler standing there. Tyler realized that it was the same old man he had seen sitting on his bed. He was the only one from the visions who ever saw him. They stared at each other for a few seconds, and then Tyler remembered what his mother had said.

And the man was just staring at me, like he wanted to talk to me.

Only he hadn't been staring at her. He was staring at Tyler behind her. And there was something else. After getting a good look at him, Tyler was frightened of what he saw.

The man looked *just* like him, only much older.

5

When Tyler woke the next morning, he could feel eyes on him. He sat up, looking first around his tiny cell, then at the surrounding cells. He saw a large black man two cells down. He was standing in his cell, facing Tyler. Just standing there, like it was his job. There hadn't been anyone in this whole cell block last night. He had to be new.

"I haven't had a chance to meet you yet, Hemingway." The man said.

"What do you mean by that, Hemingway?" Tyler said, "That's not my name."

"You were sleepin' and you kept sayin' 'it was me, I wrote the book, *I wrote the book*.'"

Tyler had been a sleep-talker his whole life. Ashleigh always joked that if he was cheating on her, he would tell on himself. He guessed that might be true.

"Oh," Tyler said. "Yeah, crazy dream. Anyways my name is Tyler."

"I think I'll stick with Hemingway," said the large man. "But my name is Bunk."

Tyler wanted to say "Top or bottom?" But he thought better of it. He had a bad habit of making jokes aloud at other people's expense, and he figured jail wasn't the right place for that., especially when the subject of the joke is the human equivalent of a Mack truck. He was probably seven feet tall, and his biceps were the size of Tyler's thighs. When Tyler didn't respond, Bunk talked for him.

"Did you really kill that woman?"

"No...I didn't. I was at home all night, passed out on the couch."

"Yeah, I ain't no Harvard man or nothin', but I saw that paper an' I said there ain't no way a man kills a woman, then writes it in the paper tellin' everyone why. It don't make sense. Unless you're crazy as hell...Are you crazy, Hemingway?"

Tyler laughed. He couldn't think of anything else to do. And he figured that maybe Bunk had his 'crazy' theory confirmed by the laugh, but he answered anyway.

"I might be, Bunk, I don't know. But I didn't kill anyone." He thought for a moment about what to say next before something dumb popped out of his mouth anyway, "What are you in for?"

He regretted asking that question immediately. He knew it was something you don't ask in jail, especially of three-hundred-pound men who could step on you. But Bunk didn't mind.

"Domestic violence," he said. "Wife got in one of those moods and had too much to drink. We got to arguin' and she slapped the piss outta me, so I hit her back. I ain't proud of it, but damn, a man can only take so much. Of course it's always the man who takes the punishment." Bunk paused for a moment, "But then there's still feminists who argue women are equal aren't there? Where are they when it comes to shit like this? I don't see anyone lobbyin' that my wife oughta be in here too, fair is fair."

"Yeah," Tyler agreed. "I guess there is an unfair double standard there."

Tyler stood up to take a piss, and Bunk respectfully turned away.

"You know, I gotta figure out who you're sposed to complain to 'round here." Said Bunk, still turned away.

"Oh yeah?" Tyler said, shaking his pecker, "For what?"

"No hot shower. No TV. It's uncomfortable as

all hell. This is the worst bed and breakfast I've ever stayed at."

Tyler laughed harder than he had in a long time. He liked Bunk's sense of humor. He was alright with him.

Not long after their conversation ended, two officers came through the doors at the end of the hallway. They approached Tyler's cell, and began unlocking it.

"You gonna be good?" One of them said to Tyler.

"A sweet little angel," he replied.

They put handcuffs on him, and started walking him down the hallway. They led him to a room on the other side of the doors they had come from. It was a familiar room, he had been here before, when Nathan disappeared. It was the interrogation room. They said for him to sit at the table, someone would be with him soon. He sat down on the cold, metal chair and waited for 'someone'.

Someone walked in the room. *Someone* was Detective Dugger.

Son of a bitch.

He strolled in the room like it was his birthday, immediately reaching up and unplugging the camera.

"I thought they only did that in movies." Tyler said.

Dugger ignored the comment and walked around to Tyler's side of the table, putting his face close to Tyler's ear.

"I got you," he said. "I finally got you, and we're going to put you *under* the fucking jail for what you did."

"I didn't kill that woman." Tyler said, but somehow he knew that wasn't what he meant. The same way that he knew what songs would be on the radio.

"I don't give a shit about that woman. I'm talking about what you did to our department, what you did to *my* operation."

Oh my God. I know what my mistake was.

"You know, I don't know how you found out about everything, or why you decided not to mention the notebook. I've thought about it for years. And I thought I had my chance to put you away three years ago when you killed your kid, but now you've gone and put yourself on a platter for me. I guess I should thank you, son. No one will believe anything you say anymore."

He's in on it! That's why he's been after me all this time. He didn't turn in the notebook because it would incriminate him.

"You're a piece of shit." Tyler told him.

Dugger bellowed out a deep, raucous laugh.

"Hey, I ain't the one who killed that poor lady, now am I?"

He walked back over to the camera in the corner of the room and plugged it back in.

"This damn thing," he muttered. "Cord is always falling out."

He turned around and walked out.

Tyler sat still and quiet. Any sane person would rat him out as soon as possible to anyone who would listen. But he had to fix the problem, and Tyler knew that meant taking him and anyone else involved with the *operation* out for good.

That night, when Tyler laid down to sleep, he concentrated on finding the hallway. He needed to speak with the Creators, to tell them that he figured out what he needed to do. He was facing the direction of his new friend, Bunk, who was snoring loudly, when he started to watch the world around him shake and vibrate as he drifted into a dream state.

He was in the corridor again. He opened a door and found the white room. He sat down at the table and waited. He knew they were watching.

"I know now," he said, "But how am I supposed to fix it from inside the prison?"

You will figure it out. But you need to hurry.

"I don't understand," he said, "I've been doing all this, for *what* reason?"

We told you. You need to fix your mistake.

"Or what?" He asked, with much frustration.

You can't afford to find out.

"What if I don't believe you? What if I don't *want* to help you?"

You will.

"Why?!" He yelled.

Because we have your son.

6

The next day, Tyler was a nervous wreck. He needed to get out, but no one had given him any information about when he could bond out, or if it was even a possibility. He didn't know if it was true that they had Nathan. If it was, why didn't they tell him sooner? It was definitely the kind of thing that would motivate him to do *anything*. But he couldn't doubt it, it *had* to be true.

"You okay, Hemingway?" Called Bunk from his cell. Tyler didn't realize he was pacing around the room so anxiously.

"No," he said.

"Wanna talk about it?"

Tyler laughed, and he noticed that Bunk seemed to take offense.

"No, I'm sorry. I really mean nothing disrespectful by what I'm about to say, but you wouldn't understand."

"Well, okay then. I'm here if you wanna talk." He said, and sat down on his bed.

"Thanks," Tyler said.

The next day was the day Ashleigh was coming to visit. The day she would bring him the book that held the answers he needed. When one o'clock came, the guards came to get Tyler from his cell. He went with them eagerly and followed them to the visitation room. He walked up to the window and saw Ashleigh sitting on the other side. She looked as if she might have aged ten years since he saw her last. Her hair was a mess, her eyes had dark circles around them.

He picked up the phone.

"Ashleigh. I can get Nathan back. I finally found out how," he said, excited.

"Tyler…"

"No, I'm serious. You have no idea what I've been going through, but I'm sure this will work, it has to. The book, it—"

"Tyler!"

"What?"

"I didn't find the book, Tyler. I searched the whole house"

Tyler's blood ran cold.

"What do you mean? It was right there on the couch!"

"But it wasn't there…and there's something else…the whole house was a mess, someone broke in Tyler. And it seems like that book is all they took."

"Damnit!" Tyler screamed. "Why can't I catch a fucking break?" He slammed the phone on the window several times, causing Ashleigh to jump back.

A guard behind Tyler who was reading a magazine looked up.

"You want to go back to your cell Roydman?" He scolded.

Tyler gritted his teeth. "Sorry, sir."

He looked back at Ashleigh, who was crying.

"Tyler," she said. "You're scaring me. Do you really think you can get him back? It's been *three years*."

"I have to try."

Ashleigh didn't know if she believed any of it, but she wanted to.

"Then let me know how I can help," she said.

Soon after his outburst, another guard came in the room and said it was time for him to return to his cell.

They told each other goodbye, and he returned to his cell.

When he got in his cell he began to kick and punch his mattress as hard as he could, screaming every obscenity he knew—nevermind Bunk who was watching the whole thing with an amused eye.

"I'm guessing she didn't find the book," said Bunk, who was staring down at the floor.

Tyler stopped.

"What did you say?"

"The book. I'm guessing she didn't find it."

Tyler turned to face Bunk. He was still staring at the floor.

"I don't remember telling you about the book," he said, each word articulated carefully.

Bunk looked up at him and smiled awkwardly.

"Yeah, man. You said you were reading this really good book, and you were going to tell your wife to bring it up here, what with you being so bored and all."

Tyler didn't remember telling him any of those things. He wasn't sure what to say.

"She's not my wife," he said, finally.

"No? My mistake. Coulda' swore that's what

you said."

"To be honest, Bunk, I don't remember discussing *any* of this with you."

Bunk stood up and walked over to the edge of his cell.

"Well maybe you said something about it in your sleep," he said. "I mean you say a lot of shit when you're sleeping." He laughed.

Tyler didn't laugh.

"Yeah," Tyler said. "Maybe."

7

Tyler tried to return to the corridor again when he was lying on his bed. He concentrated as hard as he could, picturing its winding path and ornate doors, but nothing worked. He was being blocked out somehow. He thought that if he could go there, he could find a way to escape from jail, to get out and stop Dugger and get his son back. He did manage to give himself a nosebleed though.

I'm going to give myself an aneurysm before this is over with, he thought.

He found it incredibly hard to fall asleep. All he cared about was seeing his son again. He wondered many things, like where he was being kept, was he being treated well, had he aged or not. He thought of his laugh, his smile, the way that he gave Tyler's life meaning.

Don't worry buddy, Daddy is working on it.

When his body finally gave in to sleep, he dreamt about Nathan.

He was in the operating room where Ashleigh's emergency C-section had been performed. Ashleigh was shaking uncontrollably, and there was blood everywhere. He was holding her hand as tight as he could. He smelled something burning, and heard screaming. He began to feel like he was going to be sick to his stomach. He looked at the doctor to his left, who was staring at Tyler with wide, sad eyes. He handed him a strip of gauze soaked in rubbing alcohol and instructed him to hold it to his nose and inhale. He did. The smell made him think of huffing ether as a teenager, he would get so high that it felt like tiny pixies were tickling his feet. The doctor who was performing the C-section said how this one was being stubborn. He climbed on top of the table and grabbed the baby by its legs and pulled backwards as hard as he could, like a cartoon rabbit pulling a carrot out of the ground. Tyler wanted to yell at him and tell him to be careful, but he couldn't speak. He was sedated by the staggering fumes on the gauze pad. He felt like laughing, or maybe crying, he couldn't tell. Finally, he heard a loud, exaggerated *pop!* And he saw the doctor climb off the table, holding a gray, slimy baby. The doctor handed the baby to Tyler, and, with a short laugh, he told him they did the best they could. He looked down at his lifeless son and began to scream. When he looked up, he saw that everyone in the room was laughing and cheering. Ashleigh turned to him and said that he had failed her. His eyes found the corner of the room behind her. A tall, dark figure stood there, with a featureless face, and it held its hand up to its face with long black fingers pressed to where the mouth should be in a *shhh* gesture. He looked down again at his dead baby, tears streaming from his eyes, and he began to cough uncontrollably. The baby suddenly came to life and turned his head to face Tyler. His eyes came open wide and he reached out his hand towards Tyler and spoke in a deep, haunting voice.

Come with me!
Wake up! Come with me!

Tyler's eyes were burning, he tried to look around the room but it was too hazy. The entire cellblock was filled with smoke, and the fire alarm above pulsed a bright red flash over and over as it howled, alerting everyone that there was a fire. He coughed and wheezed, choking on the foul air. He stood up and saw that he wasn't alone in his cell. Bunk stood a few feet away, the door on his cell hung wide open.

"Bunk," he shouted over the alarm, "what's going on? Did *you*—?"

"Come on!" He said. "We have to *go*!"

Bunk stepped through the open door and stormed down the hall, heading for the exit. Tyler followed him closely, shielding his eyes from the smoke as best as he could. As he passed Bunk's cell, he could see that the bars were bent outwards, as if Bunk had grabbed them and pulled them apart.

There's no way he's that strong.

When they reached the end of the hallway, Bunk touched the doorknob cautiously to feel for heat.

"Shit!" He yelled. "It's hot as all hell!"

Tyler was concentrating on opening the door with his mind, but it wasn't working. There was too much smoke, he couldn't stop choking on the fumes. He looked at Bunk, who seemed to be...vibrating.

"Step back!" Bunk said.

They both took a step back, and Bunk held out a hand in the direction of the door. All of the metal parts in the door starting shaking and clacking together loudly. The middle part of the door bowed inwards, and then, with an abrupt slamming noise, the door flung open so hard that it embedded itself into the wall.

Standing on the other side of the door were all of the guards from the jail, guns pointed at Tyler and Bunk.

"Freeze!" One of them yelled.

Tyler wasn't sure if he was speaking to them or to the fire.

Bunk waved his hand dismissively, and all three of the guard's guns flew to the west side of the room, crashing in the corner. He stepped forward and towered over the guard closest to him. The guard reached for his nightstick and Bunk swiped him out of his way like a cat playing with a mouse. The other two guards decided not to go against him, and exited the room as quickly as they could.

Bunk and Tyler ran towards the exit, and out into the parking lot. Sirens rang out from down the street, and Tyler could see a fire truck rounding the corner, with several police cruisers following.

"This way!" Bunk yelled, as he ran around the back side of the building.

Tyler followed him without question. He wanted to get out, and he had gotten his wish, it didn't matter how. They came around the back of the jail and went through a small alley, coming out on a street on the other side. Bunk was looking around, searching for something. His eyes lit up and he started running towards a green Jeep Cherokee which was parked across the street, two buildings down.

Great, so now we're going to steal a car too.

When they got to the Jeep, Bunk felt around underneath the vehicle, and pulled out a magnetic key box. He opened it, pulled out the key, and unlocked the Jeep. They both climbed in, and Bunk started the engine and began driving.

"You're a..." Tyler said, heaving from the smoke inhalation.

Bunk reached into the glove box and handed Tyler an inhaler.

"Use this." He told him.

Tyler popped the blue cap off the end of it and held it to his mouth, pressing the top down. He breathed in the cool vapors and began to feel his chest fire residing. Finally, when he felt that he could speak clearly enough, he spoke again.

"You're a Variant," he said, telling more than asking.

"Yeah," Bunk said, in a matter-of-fact sort of way.

"I'm so confused," Tyler said. "Where are we going?"

Bunk looked at him and shrugged.

"I have no idea," he said. "I don't know the area at all."

"But you're from here, right? You said you were arrested for domestic violence...because you live here...right?"

The last few words Tyler said were slower than the ones before.

"No," Bunk said, "I've never been here until a few days ago."

"Then why—"

"Look, we need somewhere to go so we can talk." Bunk said. "Obviously we can't go to your place, they're going to be looking for you there."

Tyler knew where they could go.

"My parent's house." He said.

"What? No, they'll look there too."

"Yeah, but they won't find us. My dad is some-what of a nut about government conspiracies and shit like that. He has a hidden bomb shelter with electricity, food, bathroom, everything."

"Are you sure it's hidden well?" Bunk asked him.

"Yeah," Tyler said. "Definitely. Turn right here," he said pointing to the street on their right.

As Bunk turned the vehicle, Tyler noticed he looked very worried. There were so many things he wanted to ask him, but he decided to respect Bunk's wish to wait until they were at the shelter.

They both sat in silence until Tyler would tell him to turn left here, turn right here. Finally, Bunk spoke.

"How much further?"

"Almost there."

"Are they home?"

"Should be, why?"

"They *have* to be able to keep quiet about us hiding out there. If someone comes looking, they *will* drill them for information. You think they can handle that?"

"Yeah, I mean I think so."

"You better hope so."

8

Bunk pulled the Jeep into the woods a half-mile down from Tyler's parent's house. They got out, and Bunk instructed Tyler to help him cover the Jeep with branches and brush. After they finished, Tyler stepped back and admired their work. It was obvious up close, but from the road no one would be able to see anything. Bunk reached into a backpack he had pulled from the Jeep and threw a sweatshirt and jeans at Tyler.

"Change into this," he said. "We can't go walking down the street wearing prison orange."

"Okay, yeah," Tyler said, wondering why Bunk had clothes that fit him in his car.

After they had changed, Bunk put their prison outfits into his bag and told Tyler to lead the way. As they walked down the street, Tyler prayed that no one would see them. In a quiet neighborhood like this one, two hooded men walking down the street in the early hours of the morning would draw a lot of attention. The street lamps overhead were buzzing, and Tyler was strangely comforted. He remembered playing on this very street as a kid. His mother would say, 'When the lights come on, it's time to come home.' And he was very late right now.

When they reached the house, Tyler led Bunk around the back. He figured it was better than going up to the front door, in case his parents made a scene when they answered the door. The light next to the back door was on, as always. Tyler walked over to his parent's bedroom window and tapped it lightly. He didn't want to ring the doorbell and cause a commotion. They waited a few moments to see if his parents had heard. Finally, a light came on from inside the bedroom. His father pulled back the blinds and looked at Tyler. His face held an expression of confusion mixed with horror. Tyler gestured towards the back door, and his father disappeared behind the curtains. A moment later, the door opened, and both of his parents were standing behind it.

"Tyler," his father said. "What the hell?"

"Dad, I'll explain. Can you please let us in?"

"Us?" His father said. He stuck his head out

and saw Bunk standing off to the side.

"Who is *he*?" His mother said from behind him.

"I said I'll explain, we need to get inside, please."

"Okay, okay," his father stepped aside and gestured for them to come in.

They walked inside and Tyler immediately introduced everyone.

"Bunk, this is my dad, George, and my mom, Ruth. Guys, this is Bunk."

Bunk reached out to shake their hands, but neither of them took it.

"Listen, he's helping me," he said.

"Helping you with what?" George said, "Escape from jail? Jesus, and you guys smell like a bonfire, what the hell is going on?"

Ruth stepped between them and looked her son in the eyes.

"Tyler, please tell me you didn't do it." She said with tears in her eyes.

"No, mom. I didn't. That's what I'm telling you guys. We need to use the shelter for a while, until this blows over. I'll explain everything as soon as possible. Is that okay?" He said, looking at his father.

"You really are innocent, aren't you?" George said, frowning.

"Yes, dad."

"You still know how to get in there? The way I showed you?"

"Yeah."

"Okay," he said, putting a hand on his shoulder. "But in the morning, we want answers."

"Just please, if they come looking here…you never saw us."

"Of course," George said.

Tyler led Bunk out to the shed behind the house. He lifted the wooden handle and pulled the door towards him, which came open with a thud. When they stepped inside, they turned on the lights. The shed was full of boxes, old chairs, and plastic storage totes.

"Some apocalypse shelter," Bunk said.

"This isn't it," said Tyler. "I told you it's legit. Check this out."

He walked to the center of the room and pulled one of the boards up. Underneath it was a keypad and a lever shaped like an arrow—the same kind you would expect to find on a safe. He pressed six numbers on the keypad, and it beeped three times.

He pulled the lever to the right, and it clicked, allowing them entry.

"Damn," Bunk said from behind him, sounding impressed.

"Yeah. Told you," Tyler said.

He lifted the handle, and the hatch opened up to a staircase leading down below ground. He motioned for Bunk to go first, and Bunk began walking down the stairs. Tyler followed him and turned around once his head was clear of the door, pressing a button on the wall. The hatch closed slowly, and he heard a click, indicating that it was locked. Tyler turned around and followed Bunk down the stairs and into the bunker, fluorescent lights lighting their path. When they reached the bottom, they admired the room. The entire left wall was stocked with food and bottled water. The right wall had a television, bookshelves, and a treadmill. There were two couches in the middle of the room which folded out into beds, and there was a table with four chairs behind the couch. The back of the room had a bathroom with a working toilet and shower. Tyler looked at Bunk to see his expression.

"Okay," Bunk said, smiling as he threw up his hands. "You were right."

9

Tyler and Bunk agreed that they both needed a shower. The smoke smell on them was overwhelming. Tyler showed Bunk where to find the towels, and Bunk thanked him and closed the bathroom door. Tyler went to sit on the couch and turned on the television. He didn't find any news stories about the jail catching fire, not yet anyways. He settled for a strange, late hours cartoon and waited for Bunk to finish. A few minutes later, he came out of the bathroom.

"I'm glad I smell better, but damn these clothes still reek!" He said.

Tyler laughed as he got up to take his turn in the bathroom. After he was finished, he returned to the main room.

"You hungry?" He asked.

"Starvin'," Bunk replied.

"Yeah, me too. Let's see what we can find." Tyler said, walking to the wall of food.

They both claimed some food for themselves, as well as a bottle of water each, and sat down at the table. Tyler was extremely anxious to get some answers. Bunk looked up at him, and stared for a moment.

"What?" Tyler said.

"Nothing," Bunk said. "Well, not nothing. It's just that now that I get a good look at you, I know for sure."

"Know *what?*"

"That you're him."

"I'm who?"

"The one who wrote the book."

"You're going to have to help me out here."

Bunk leaned back in his seat. "Alright man, I guess there's a lot you don't know. I'll tell you everything I know, hopefully it helps."

Tyler nodded.

"How much do you know about Variants?" Bunk asked.

"Almost nothing," Tyler said. "I just heard the word for the first time recently."

"From the Creators?"

"Yeah."

"Okay well, here goes. Ever since I was little, I could *change* certain things. I'd get these urges like something bad was about to happen, and I would somehow have the ability to change them for the better. And every time, I would get these—"

"Nosebleeds."

"Yeah," Bunk said. "So yeah, here's the part you don't know. An old man came to me and he told me that our universe is in trouble. He said that he needed to contact you, but he wasn't able to find you. He told me that he wrote a book and hid it somewhere where you would know to find it, he was sure about that. But he also said that the Creators were hellbent on making sure you don't read what was in it. That's why he sent me. At first, I thought he was an old quack, but he knew too much about Variants for me not to listen to him. All my life I've been thinking I was crazy and that there was no way I was actually doing the things I thought I was. But then someone comes around and starts telling me that he knows about my powers and all that, so I had to listen."

Tyler sat in silence for a moment before speaking. "So, what was in the book?"

"I don't know. All he could tell me was that you would be in jail for something you didn't do, and that I was the key to helping you to get out and fix everything. So I drove up here and got myself arrested. Made up the story about domestic violence. I've never even set foot in Minnesota before, and I'm not even married."

"Are you the one who has been contacting me? From Alabama?"

"Yeah, the old man has been contacting me for a while now. He told me about your son. He said that the Creators do not mean well. They have no intentions of giving him back. They just want your help. They can be masters of deceit."

"But I *can* get him back, right?"

"The old man told me that it's up to *you* to save your son. I guess it was outlined in the book. But somehow he knew that they would take the book. It doesn't make sense to me."

"So what did you mean that I was him?" Tyler asked.

"Well, like I said, when I got myself in the jail, I knew that you were the one I needed to help. But when I saw your face, I thought you looked an awful lot like the old man, only younger of course. But then you were saying 'I wrote the book' over and over in your dream. It all made sense. It's why the old man knew so much about you, and your son, and how to fix everything. It's because he already lived your life, and he knows how to fix it. It's because he's you."

Tyler sighed. He did already know this, but it just didn't seem believable. When would he discover time travel? And if the old version of himself knows how to fix everything, why didn't he?

"Did he...did *I* tell you more about the Creators? I don't know anything about them other than what they told me. That they created everything, and that Variants change things, and that I messed something up which had to be fixed." Tyler said.

"From what I understand," Bunk began, "well from what *you* told me, in the very beginning of the universe, Creators and Variants were equals. The Creators were supposed to watch over the world and see that things went as they were supposed to, and the Variants were placed randomly throughout the world to act as regulators of events. Think of it as a checks and balances system. Creators can't have too much power because they can't physically harm a Variant. But there's a problem. Creators *can* harm or influence normal people. Supposedly, the Creators started getting power hungry and wanted to rid the world of all Variants, got tired of things changing that they had no control over. That's all I really know."

Tyler pushed his food away from him and stood up, backing away from the table. He began to pace the room.

"So," he said. "If our universe is in trouble, and I'm the only one who can fix it, then I have leverage over the Creators, right?"

"You would think so."

"Do *you* think so?"

"What are you getting at?" Bunk said, looking confused.

"Well, as far as my son goes. You said that they have no intention of giving him back, why even take him then?"

Bunk thought for a moment. He could tell that Tyler would do anything to get his son back, but he didn't know if he believed that he could.

"I don't know, but we have to try. Let's start by saving the universe, what do you say? Wonder twin powers activate?" Bunk smiled and held out his fist in Tyler's direction.

"Yeah," Tyler said, bumping Bunk's fist with his own. "Wonder twin powers activate."

10

For the next few hours, Tyler told Bunk about how he had saved Laura Leigh from Officer Mills. He told him about the notebook, and how Dugger had kept it secret, how he had told Tyler that he had been trying to get him for years for ruining *his* operation.

"So," Bunk said, "you're sure that this is the mistake you're supposed to fix?"

"As sure as I can be," Tyler replied. "I mean, he made it obvious that he was in on it. My guess is, Dugger was working with Mills. It's possible he's been continuing the...legacy to this day."

"Jesus."

"Yeah. I don't know why I didn't think to do something about it. After that night I just felt glad that I had saved that girl's life, ya know? Never occurred to me that my job wasn't done."

"Well now we can finish it. Fuck this guy," said Bunk. "Do you have a plan?"

"Does 'find him and kill him' count as a plan?"

"Sure does."

"You know," Tyler began, "you don't have to help me. You've helped enough as it is."

"But I do," Bunk said. "The same way you had to help that girl. I need to do this. And I want to."

Just then, a noise came from up the stairs. It was the door opening. They both looked around for a weapon of some sort, just in case.

"It's me," came George's voice from the top of the stairs. He walked down to the bottom. "They've already been here," he said.

Bunk and Tyler exchanged glances.

"Really?" said Tyler. "What happened?"

"They came knocking on our door about six this morning, saying that you had escaped jail, and did we know anything, and that you and the other guy were very dangerous."

"What did you say?" Tyler asked.

"I said how I haven't seen or talked to my son in months, how he had kept to himself lately," George looked at the floor when he said the last part.

Tyler felt a sting of guilt. It was almost the whole truth. He *hadn't* talked to his parents in months. It was too hard to face them after he lost Nathan under his care.

"So do you think they believed it?"

"I don't know. But they didn't ask to look around, not yet anyways. Guy gave me a card though, said for me to call him if I saw you guys." He handed the card to Tyler.

Tyler read the name on the card.

Det. William Dugger

There was a phone number below.

"You guys ready to tell me what the heck is going on?"

Tyler nervously flicked the business card between his fingers. He wasn't sure if he should tell his father the truth. What would happen if a normal person learned about Variants? Would it even matter? He decided to stick as close to the truth as possible, without going into too much detail.

"Why don't you have a seat, dad."

George sat down and pulled out a pack of Camel cigarettes. He pulled one out and started to put the pack back into his jacket pocket, but then he pulled out two more and handed one each to Tyler and Bunk.

Tyler took his cigarette cautiously, like an animal taking food from a stranger.

"Oh come on, Tyler," George said. "You think I'm stupid? I found your menthols in your car on more than one occasion when you still lived here. We're all adults, right?"

He reached back into his pocket and produced a lighter, passing it around.

"Okay," Tyler said, finally after inhaling a drag from the cigarette. "Do you remember the incidents I would have as a kid. With the nosebleeds?"

"Yeah, how could I forget? We thought you had something bad wrong with you."

"Well the nosebleeds were always accompanied by something else. It's hard to explain." Tyler was still unsure of how far he should take this. His eyes glanced over at Bunk who had an expression on his face that said *I don't see what it could hurt to tell him.*

"I'm listening," George said.

"It's going to sound crazy," Tyler said, "but I know when certain things will happen—bad things—and I am able to change them. Like with the school bus, you remember that, right?"

"Yeah, almost crashed into the house." George ran his hand through the little bit of hair he had nervously.

"I kept it from crashing, dad. I don't know how I do it, but when I need to do it, it just comes to me."

"And the girl in that cop's basement?"

"That too. I was led there, had one of my feelings, and I drove straight to that prick's house."

George pulled three more cigarettes out, passing them around like Halloween candy. "This seems...I don't know Tyler, this is too much."

Bunk spoke for the first time in a while. "It's true Mr. Roydm—"

"George."

"George," Bunk continued, "it's true. I can do the same things."

George sat back in his chair and took a long drag on his cigarette.

"You know," he began, "I've always kind of known that you were special, Tyler. It was hard to ignore when you were growing up. But how do you rationalize something like this to yourself? You don't. You *have* to ignore it, because it *can't* be true. At least that's what I thought." He sighed.

"I didn't even know what I..." Tyler searched for the right word, "what I *was*, what I *am,* until just recently. The word for it is Variant. Bunk is one too. We have these...abilities because we're supposed to be here to bring order to the universe, to keep things from happening that aren't supposed to. And I learned something else, dad."

"What?"

"That there's still a chance to get Nathan back."

"Tyler..."

"I'm serious." Tyler said, and Bunk nodded in agreement.

"Ok then," George looked even more skeptical now as he asked, "how do you do that?"

"I'm working on that right now. By the way, where's mom? I know she's dying to hear all of this."

"She's keeping watch. In case they come back looking again. I'm sure they suspect us."

"Well, I'm sorry I put you guys in this position. Just didn't know where else to go."

George stood up and walked over to the wall of food, nervously shuffling things around.

"You're not putting us in any position, son," he said, still turned away. "Just make sure you get my grandson back, and make sure whoever took him pays dearly." He turned around and faced them.

"It was nice meeting you," he said to Bunk.

And he walked up the stairs and left the shelter.

After the hatch at the top of the stairs was completely shut, Bunk glanced in Tyler's direction.

"That was weird."

"Yeah."

"I can't believe you told him all that, and he seemed to just…believe it. What kind of person just takes crazy shit like this like it's normal, every day conversation?"

Tyler looked up towards the hatch his father had exited from. "The kind of person who builds a secret bomb shelter in their backyard, I guess. And I think he just *wants* to believe it, the part about getting Nathan back anyways. He loved that kid so much. I mean when I was growing up he did the best he could to be a good dad, but we didn't always have the best relationship. I think he saw my son as a chance to try again, you know?"

"I can relate to that," Bunk said. "I mean, I don't have kids or anything, but me and my dad definitely had it rough, as in black eyes at least twice a year."

Tyler suddenly felt silly by comparison. He certainly had never had such an experience with his dad. "I'm sorry," he said. "I definitely think you've got me beat there."

"Yeah. Well I wasn't the best kid either," he sighed and thought for a moment. "Anyways, I guess we've waited long enough. Where do we start?"

"My gun," Tyler said. "I need to get my gun."

11

Tyler didn't want to sleep, but he could tell that Bunk was exhausted. They each took a couch and laid down to take a nap. Tyler stared up at the ceiling of the bunker, and found comfort in their current safe place. Safe felt good, but it couldn't last forever. Nothing good ever did. Unless your idea of good is a shitstorm, in which case, everything good will last forever, yay!

When he finally fell asleep, he didn't dream at all. He was hoping to find the corridor again, to have any more information from the Creators, but he wasn't able to get there. He woke when he heard Bunk stirring. He looked around the room and saw him packing some supplies into his pack. Bunk looked up at Tyler.

"Hope he won't mind."

"He won't," Tyler replied.

He stood up and stretched. How long had they slept? It didn't feel like long.

"Sorry if I woke you," said Bunk.

"No, it's okay. We need to get going."

"It's almost dark now. I went up and checked about half an hour ago. I think we need to move in the dark."

Tyler agreed. He walked over to where Bunk was standing and helped him pack.

"Hey man," Tyler began, "I just want you to know how serious this is, what we're about to do."

"We don't have a choice."

"I know, I just hope we're ready."

Once it was dark they left the shelter and went into the back door of Tyler's parent's house. He hugged them both, and they wished them luck. Ruth was crying silently. Tyler told them not to worry—a waste of breath, but it needed to be said—and they left. They went back down the street cautiously again, as to not be seen, and made their way into the woods where Bunk's vehicle was still safely hidden. They removed the branches and brush that was covering it and climbed inside.

"Alright," Bunk said. "We know they are more than likely watching your house. So we will need a distraction. Something big, to make any cop within a ten mile radius respond."

Tyler nodded in agreement.

They drove for a few minutes before Bunk asked the question he had been wanting to ask Tyler for a while. There was something obvious burning in the back of his mind he had wanted to say, but for some reason he had decided not to say until right now.

"Why *your* gun?"

Tyler sat in thought for a moment.

"I don't know. I just feel like I *need* it."

"Yeah but doesn't your dad have a gun? I mean why risk getting caught going to your house?"

"It's like how you said you *need* to help me. I know I need my gun. I can't explain it. Maybe it's a...Variant thing. Besides, I don't want anything we do connected to anyone else."

"Yeah," Bunk said. "I guess you're right about that."

"Turn in here," Tyler told him, pointing at the gas station down the street from his house.

"You gonna buy a candy bar or something?"

"No, I need some cigarettes. You want anything?"

"We do need some gas," Bunk realized.

"Good."

Bunk pulled up to the pump, and Tyler got out and started pumping while he went inside to pay for the gas. They realized they couldn't use cards, didn't need them being tracked. But Tyler still couldn't help thinking of what Ashleigh would always say about pre-paying for gas.

The last dollar is almost all air.

He thought of how the last *whatever* was usually a bitter disappointment. The last kiss. *The Last Airbender.* The last bite of that McDonald's Cheeseburger. Hell, maybe it was the realization that your tasty cow was probably a sweetheart before it was slaughtered for your pleasure. Whatever it was, lasts weren't usually good, and for Detective William Dugger, his last of days was approaching fast.

"The fuck are you *doing?*" Bunk said from behind him.

Tyler hadn't realized until now that he was so deep in thought, that the gas tank had overflowed and was spilling out in a puddle all around the car, and causing a small river to run through the parking lot.

I'm losing it.

"I don't know. I was just thinking about things, and aren't these things supposed to have stoppers or something to keep that from happening?"

"Yeah man, it's called your brain." Bunk laughed, stepped over the small river of gasoline, and got in the car, holding a soda and some gummy worms.

Tyler walked inside the gas station and went into the bathroom. It was a dingy little hole, and it smelled like a dumpster that might sit outside of a clinic where they perform colonoscopies. There was one urinal and one stall in the bathroom, and the stall was currently occupied by a man who was seemingly dying on the toilet of bowel pain.

"Oh! God!" The man in the stall said to the walls, or to Tyler, he wasn't sure.

Tyler hastily began to wash his hands, even though he knew the gasoline smell would linger longer than any person could ever dream it would.

"You know what they always say!" The man in the stall droned on. "When you gotta go—"

Unreasonably long and boisterous fart.

"—you gotta go!"

Tyler was trying not to puke as he reached for a paper towel but there were none in the dispenser.

Wiping my hands on my pants it is, he thought with a shrug.

He bolted out of the door and walked to the candy section, grabbing some circus peanuts. He grabbed a drink from the coolers and approached the checkout counter. The woman's name tag said that her name was Denise.

"The hell is that smell?" Denise said, chewing gum.

Tyler looked around the room, making sure she wasn't talking to someone else.

"If it smells like death, it's probably Hoss in the bathroom there, giving it all he's got," he said, pointing to the men's room.

"No," Denise said. "It's *you*. You're covered in gas!" Her upper lip curled up. It would reach the heavens if only her face would allow it.

"Oh," Tyler said. "Yeah, accident. Anyway I'll take a pack of Camel menthols and a small lighter, please."

Denise snorted as she reached for Tyler's cigarettes. Tyler could see her tramp stamp tattoo as she bent over. It was literally the word "TRAMP" stamped right there over her ass. Tyler wasn't sure if this was great humor, or even greater self-deprecation. She turned around and gave Tyler his total, and he paid her.

"I know who you are," said Denise as Tyler turned to walk away. "When I saw your buddy from *The Green Mile* walk in here, I thought I recognized him, but then you walked in here too. You're all over the news for what you did. Maybe I'll call the cops," she said. "Maybe I won't." Her eyebrows raised in accusatory fashion.

"You don't know what you're talking about." Tyler said.

"Oh really? So, your license *didn't* say Tyler Roydman just then, when you paid me? And it *wasn't* caught on camera?"

Shit.

She continued, "and let me tell you, I *need* that reward money. I think I *will* call them." She snickered.

How could he be so stupid.

"What do you want...to keep quiet?" Tyler asked her, annoyance heavy in his voice.

"Well, the reward money is one thousand. So, I'm thinking...two."

"You want me to give you two thousand dollars?"

"That's what I said. Or you're fucked, buddy." She let out a quick laugh.

"I'll be right back," Tyler told her.

As he walked outside, he looked around the parking lot. It was empty except for three cars. There was Bunk's Jeep, and two more which Tyler assumed belonged to Denise and Hoss from the men's. He unwrapped the plastic from his pack of cigarettes and pulled one out, smelling the menthol. He stuck one in his mouth and lit it with the small blue lighter Denise had sold him. He looked inside, and Denise pointed at her imaginary watch on her wrist as if to say *Clock's ticking, I'm gonna call even if you do give me money and get three thousand, douchebag.*

He walked over to the Jeep and climbed in the passenger seat, still holding the cigarette in his mouth.

"Whoa," said Bunk. "It's whatever if you want to kill yourself with those things, but not in the Jeep, man."

"Relax," he said, looking forward."Just drive."

Bunk sighed and drove towards the exit, and as he pulled out onto the street, Tyler flicked his cigarette behind them, igniting the river of gasoline, the trail of fire raging it's path right up to the pump Tyler left on the ground.

12

Betty Lynn Mcgowan was sitting in her rocking chair, knitting a scarf for an unknown future recipient. The man on the television was droning on about how there was a psychotic murderer running loose with a criminal sidekick in Monticello. He said they were highly dangerous and were believed to be traveling in a green Jeep. Betty laughed at the TV.

"A green Jeep," she muttered.

The thing about Betty Lynn Mcgowan was that she hadn't been of right mind for years, and no one in her family had decided to take responsibility for her. So there she sat, day after day, knitting and pissing herself mostly. She would of course eat and sleep, but not much else. And since she hadn't been a problem to any neighbors, she was able to just go on living that way. Her bills all came straight out of her checking account automatically. The same account that her social security check was deposited into monthly. On this particular evening, she was watching the news as she usually did, when she heard and felt a thunderous, earth-shattering *BOOM*.

At first, Betty thought of terrorists. There were terrorists everywhere. Ever since they did that thing in New York, it was only a matter of time until they hit closer to home. But no, Betty had a feeling it was something else. Finally, the rapture. She began to sing absentmindedly.

I looked over Jordan and what did I see?
Commin' for to carry me home.
There was a band of angels a-commin' after me.
Commin' for to carry me home.
Swing low, sweet chariot.
Commin' for to carry me home.
Swing low, sweet chariot.
Commin' for to carry me home.

She walked over to the window and looked out. There was a blazing inferno outside. And the *heat*. The heat from outside her window was unbearable.

"Oh sweet Jesus, it's not you!" She said. "It's the Devil himself out there! Oh bless us all!"

She walked slowly over to the old rotary dial

telephone hanging on the wall and picked up the receiver. She put her finger in the hole for "9" then "1" then "1" again. When the operator picked up, Betty was in tears.

"Hello? I said what is your emergency? Hello?"

"Satan," Betty Lynn said. "Satan is loose on Broad Street."

13

Bunk wheeled the Jeep around the corner as fast as it would go, the tires screeching furiously.

"Are you fuckin' crazy?" He yelled, glancing at the blaze in the rearview mirror.

Tyler didn't respond. Bunk looked over at him and saw that he was shaking violently.

"Tyler!" He shouted. "You having a seizure?"

He pulled the Jeep over on the side of the road as two police cruisers zoomed by with their sirens blaring. He turned on the overhead light and saw that Tyler's nose was bleeding down the front of his shirt. He was a mess. Tyler snapped into reality and looked at Bunk with wide, confused eyes. Bunk handed him an old t-shirt he found in the backseat and told him to wipe his face. Tyler took the shirt and pulled his visor down to see his nose.

"It just happened." Tyler said. "Just like all the other times."

"I don't know if Variants are supposed to go around blowing up gas stations, Tyler. I don't think that's the type of change we're supposed to bring."

"She was trying to stop what we are doing. She was going to call the cops. Besides, we don't know that anyone died."

"The whole building went up. I'm pretty sure anyone inside is dead."

There was an uncomfortable feeling of dread in the air. They both knew they were on a mission of sorts, and that the whole world depended on Tyler fixing his mistake, but neither of them were prepared for *this*.

"I don't know what to say," Tyler said. "I guess something about omelettes and breaking eggs."

Bunk snorted. "You got a fucked up way of viewing the world," he said.

He pulled the Jeep back onto the road. "One thing's for sure," he continued. "Ain't no cops gonna be at your house."

They drove a bit further down the road, and Tyler motioned for Bunk to pull into his driveway. The area looked clear, but he still told him to park behind the house to be sure they wouldn't be seen by cars passing by.

"Wait here," he said as he got out of the Jeep. "I won't be long." He shut the door and walked to the back of the house. He moved around some rocks and found the fake one with the hide-a-key. He used the key on the back door and stepped inside. Right inside the door was his washer and dryer. How he wished he could clean his clothes right now, but they didn't need to stay long.

He walked into the hallway, stopping to glance into Nathan's room. Memories of his son flooded into his mind: reading to him, chasing him around laughing, and even his earliest weeks when he would wake up at two in the morning and need a diaper change and a bottle. What used to be an annoyance now seemed like the most desirable thing he could imagine, to wake up and know that your baby *needs* you, and to be able to give him what he needs. To smell his head and know that he is yours.

"Not long now, bud," said Tyler to the empty room.

He continued down the hallway and into the living room. He could tell that someone had been here, possibly a lot of people. The cushions had been removed from the couch and stacked in the corner, the cabinets in the kitchen were all open, and the computer was gone.

"Jesus," Tyler said to himself.

He wondered if it was the cops, or if he had been robbed. Or could it have been the Creators looking for the book? There was no way to be sure. He began to doubt that his gun would even be there. When he walked into his bedroom, he opened his sock drawer and checked for the gun anyway. It was there, right where he always kept it. He picked it up and he also grabbed a box of 9mm rounds and turned around to face the bed. The bed where he used to make love to Ashleigh. It seemed so long ago, but the memories had not left him. He used to love it when she would pull him close to her and put his arm around her, laying her head on his chest. It was better than sex, it was love. But for him, nothing great lasted long. It was true what they said about true love only existing in fairy tales.

He took one last glance around the bedroom and turned around to step back into the living room. When he turned around, he wanted to scream. He wanted to scream and run and cry but he couldn't move. Standing halfway across the room, behind the couch, was a tall, dark figure with no face and long, black fingers.

Creator.

Tyler was unable to move, unable to speak, he was frozen in place—paralyzed. The creature stared at Tyler for what seemed like an eternity before speaking. When it spoke, there was no mouth to deliver the words, no eyes to deliver emotion. It was as if it spoke directly into Tyler's brain.

What is it that you are waiting for? The creature said to him, its voice raspy, yet wispy.

Tyler could feel his hands trembling as his body struggled against its inability to move or speak. He wasn't sure if it was out of fear or true incapacitation.

Speak, Variant.

"...I..I...." Tyler stumbled.

The creature waved it's arm over it's head and muttered something quietly. It then pointed at Tyler slowly and seemed to jab him from across the room. Tyler suddenly found himself able to speak.

"I have been trying as hard as I can to do what you want. Don't you think I have a reason to figure this out?"

The creature turned it's head the way a dog does when you talk to it with a funny voice. It turned it again, this time to the other side.

If you don't act soon, there will be nothing.

The room went completely black as all the lights in the house went out. Tyler fell down to his knees as if he had been suddenly released by a giant's grip. He panted heavily as he stood up and reached for the light switch. He flipped the switch and looked around the house. No one else was there with him. He rushed to the back of the house holding the gun out in front of him like his dick at a urinal. He exited through the back door, locking it behind him. He placed the hide-a-key back in its place, and got in the Jeep.

14

Ashleigh stood in her kitchen and stared at the television in disbelief. Pieces of what the news anchors were saying were floating through the air like ash from a bonfire, but only some of them were hitting her.

Roydman.

Explosion.

MURDER.

She was on her fourth glass of wine already, and she was ill prepared to cope with this nonsense. She suddenly wished she could help Tyler—to join him in finding Nathan. Even though she believed that to be nearly impossible, she still had hope. She had to believe in something. Since she had returned from her visit with Tyler at the jail, she had the feeling of being watched. She had even noticed the same van parked outside of her house on several occasions. She remembered Tyler would say that stereotypes were all based on small truths. She wondered if the same was true of paranoia. After finishing the last sip of wine from her glass, she walked to the sink and sat the glass on the edge.

I may want more later.

She turned and stepped carefully into the living room, swaying a little with each step, and grabbed the remote for the TV. The story of her ex-husband's maniacal, murderous rampage through town was being replayed continuously, and she was tired of hearing it. Usually Ashleigh would leave the TV on, even if it was muted. It kept her from feeling so alone, even if only slightly. But at this particular moment she had no desire for anything that loud or that bright. Her head felt like a balloon that was inflated past its limits, ready to pop. She felt for the large red button at the top of the remote, and pressed it, turning the TV off. The screen turned a glossy black, and she noticed a dark version of her reflection looking back at her. But there was something else. Something was *moving* behind her. She screamed as she watched a tall figure reach its long black fingers towards her neck. She wielded the remote in her hand, and turned around to use it as a weapon. It was her only option—to fight. But when she turned around, there was nothing behind her.

Her heart raced in her chest, and she felt a surge of blood rush through her veins. She was a raging force of adrenaline, ready to strike. She quickly walked over to the kitchen drawer and pulled out a large knife. Her breath was coming in short, harsh bursts, and she had to remind herself to take them. She walked around the corner from the kitchen and turned to go down the hallway. She was going to check every room. She had seen something, and she meant to destroy it. She stopped after every couple of steps and looked around, making sure nothing was about to grab her. She approached the first door on her left—the bathroom door—and reached for the handle. Slowly, she turned the handle and peeked inside, knife at the ready. Nothing. Just as she closed the door back, the doorbell rang, causing her to jump and squeal. She turned her body to face the door while simultaneously keeping a stark awareness of what could be behind her.

"Who is it?" She asked the door.

"Police," was the reply.

She walked over to the blinds and flipped them down with her index and middle finger. There was a Monticello PD squad car in the lot. She walked over to the door and pulled the chain away. Slowly, she opened the door and saw that there were two officers standing on the other side of it. The officer on the left was a tall, lanky man with a nametag reading "Holt," and the other was a shorter, fat man named Grier.

"Ma'am," Holt began, "D'ya mind putting that down?" He gestured towards her hand. She had forgotten that she was still wielding a knife from the kitchen.

"I'm sorry, I…well I saw something in the apartment. In my TV screen, it was behind me."

"You saw something on TV and grabbed a knife?"

"No!" Ashleigh said, much louder than she had planned. "I saw the *reflection* of something in the TV, so I grabbed the knife."

"You been drinkin' ma'am?" Grier asked, stepping forward.

"Is it a crime to have a glass of wine in your own place now?" Ashleigh asked. "Besides, I know what I saw. You'd be surprised at how quickly you sober up when you see what I saw."

"Well I guess we can take a look around for you while we're here, ease your mind?"

"Please do." Ashleigh said. "And then maybe

you can tell me why you're here."

The two officers stepped inside and checked every room in the apartment for any unwelcome intruders. After a couple of minutes they returned to Ashleigh, who was sitting on the couch with her knees drawn to her chest.

"There's nothing here," Holt reported as they returned to the living room.

Ashleigh sat forward and looked at him as if she was thinking hard about what to say next. She opened her mouth to speak, and then closed it, frowning.

Officer Holt spoke for her.

"We came here because we wanted to ask you some questions, if you don't mind."

"About Tyler."

"Well…yes. Of course you know we have to find out what we can. I understand that you have been separated for years, but I also know that you visited him in jail. Surely you can understand why we feel we have to ask what you know?"

"Yes, I understand. Yeah I visited him. Only because he asked for me to. I don't hate Tyler just because we're not together you know."

"But have you seen him since he escaped? The

whole town—hell, the whole *state* is in an uproar with a murderer on the loose."

Officer Grier interrupted the conversation by asking if it was okay if he used her coffeemaker. She said that it was and quickly turned back to face Holt.

"No, I haven't seen him. And he is *not* a murderer."

"Oh, come on now, he confessed in the papers. We all saw it. He even told us how and why he did it!"

Ashleigh's grip on the edge of the couch tightened.

"Is that why you're here?" She asked, her throat dry. "To tell me what you believe Tyler did? How do we know he wasn't set up?" She was on her feet now, staring into Holt's eyes.

Holt returned her stare, and for a moment which lasted far longer than Ashleigh was comfortable with, nobody spoke. Finally, Officer Grier returned to the room and handed a cup of coffee to Ashleigh and sat down on the chair across from her, cradling his own cup of coffee in his hands.

"Please, sit," Grier said, smiling. "We have a lot to discuss."

Ashleigh shot a glance at Holt as she sat down and took a sip from her coffee. It was bitter and unpleasant. She wasn't much of a fan of coffee, but it couldn't hurt to sober up a little.

"Ask away," she said, throwing her hands up.

Officer Holt slowly stood up and pulled a small legal pad out of his pocket.

"Well," he began, "I wanted to start by saying how savuhshuhniah."

"W…what?"

"I said how suhvghhh."

Ashleigh started rubbing her eyes. Everything was blurry and sounds were warped. She looked down at her coffee.

"Mother….fuhh." She tried to finish the curse but was unsuccessful.

She was losing consciousness but was able to tell that the two officers were mocking her, dancing around the room and laughing. Reality and fantasy started blending together as Robin Williams screamed *Good Morning Vietnam!* From somewhere in the room.

I'm going to die. I'm going to die and they're laughing.

"Come on in, boss, she's ready." Ashleigh heard Holt say into his radio.

She struggled against the chemicals which were raging inside of her, but it was pointless. She looked down at the floor which was currently turning into quicksand. She leaned over the couch and began falling. She fell, and fell, and fell again through the quicksand. She heard boots enter the room, seemingly from about five miles away. Of course she wasn't falling in quicksand; she was slumped on the floor with her ass in the air and one of her legs still on the couch. The floor seemed to rumble and shake as footsteps drew the figure nearer to her. The last thing she saw before sleep took her was Detective Dugger leaning over her to tie her hands behind her back.

15

Bunk looked at Tyler when he got back into the passenger seat of the Jeep.

"Well? Did you get it?"

Tyler looked at him slowly, as if he hadn't noticed Bunk had spoken.

"What?"

"The gun. Did you get the gun?" Bunk looked annoyed.

"Oh...yeah," Tyler said, pulling the Glock out of his waistband and feeling the smooth metal on his skin. "Listen, something happened in there. I saw one of the Creators. He told me if I didn't act soon, there would be nothing."

"What the fuck? What did you do?"

"I couldn't *do* anything. I was frozen, couldn't even move my arms." Tyler said. "I mean, I told them I was trying to do what they want, but they won't leave me alone."

"It just doesn't make sense," Bunk said. "And what happens if killing this Dugger guy doesn't do anything? Then what? We've gone and murdered a cop."

"I told you already that you could back out."

"No, I mean I came all the way up here to help, not to run. It's just hard not to have some doubts, you know?"

"Trust me, I do."

"So what now?" Bunk asked, unsure of where to go. They were still parked behind Tyler's house.

"I don't know, but I have an idea." Tyler said, reaching into his pocket and pulling out a business card. "We need to find a phone."

16

Ruth Roydman almost choked on her coffee as she read the *Monticello Times*.

"George! George come here!"

Footsteps rang out as George hurried down the stairs.

"What is it? Everything okay?" He called out.

"Look," she told him pointing at the front page.

George picked up the paper and mouthed silently as he read the story, a look of shock mixed with anger painted on his face.

"They won't get away with this," he said finally.

"I hope you're right," Ruth said. "But they're saying Tyler kidnapped or killed Ashleigh now, everyone will believe it, they've got everyone believing everything they say about him." She sat back in her chair and slammed her fists onto the table. "What do you do when the police are out to get you? When the good guys turn into the bad guys?" She asked.

"Well," George said, setting the paper down. "I guess you fight back."

17

Tyler and Bunk had begun driving in no particular direction. They had to keep moving. Tyler was holding Detective Dugger's business card in between his fingers, playing with the edges. He was wondering if he would have any trouble doing it— ending Dugger. Before he could tell Bunk to look for a payphone, he heard a cell phone ring. It was one of those generic, loud ringtones. Bunk shot a glance at Tyler that said *I thought you didn't have a phone?*

"I don't know what the hell that is," Tyler said, looking for the source of the noise. He started digging through the backpack his father had given him to put supplies in. After digging for a few seconds, he found the source of the ringing. There was a small flip phone in the bottom of the bag. He flipped it open.

"...Hello?" he said. Bunk gave Tyler a puzzled look.

"It's dad," said George Roydman.

"Dad...what's going on? What's the deal with the phone?"

"I put it in the bag. It's just a cheap phone I picked up at the store. I slipped it in the bag because I knew you would need it. I don't know why I didn't tell you about it, I guess it just figured you might think I was babying you."

"No, dad. Not at all. Thank you." Tyler said, genuinely thankful. He felt tears welling up in his eyes, and he couldn't have explained why.

"Things aren't looking good, are they?"

"Besides the obvious?"

"Oh, you don't know do you? Of course you don't.."

"Don't know what, dad?"

"I don't know how to tell you, Tyler. All of this, it's just too much."

"Just tell me!" Tyler said, frustrated.

"Well...it would appear that you've taken Ashleigh now. At least that's what the papers are reporting."

There was silence on the line and for a moment the only noise was the wind outside the Jeep, and Tyler's unsteady breathing. Thoughts were racing in his mind, and he found it hard to concentrate.

"Tyler?"

"Yeah. I'm here."

"There's something you should know," George said. "The officer who handled the crime scene at Ashleigh's apartment *found* your DNA everywhere. It was Dugger."

But George didn't have to tell Tyler who it was. They told each other goodbye and Tyler told Bunk what his father had told him.

"What do we do?" Bunk asked.

"We need to find out where he lives. He may be keeping her somewhere on his property, like Mills was doing."

Bunk thought for a moment.

"Phone book?" He suggested.

Tyler called his dad back and asked him to check the phone book for the address of William Dugger. Tyler wrote down the address on his hand and after hanging up the phone, he told Bunk.

"800 Andrews Drive. I know exactly where that is," Tyler said.

"Just tell me where to go." Bunk said with a smile.

Both of them were exhausted. The little bit of

sleep they got at the bunker had worn off and they were running on fumes, but they had to press on. They drove to 800 Andrews Drive and parked at the road. Tyler chambered a bullet in the Glock and looked at Bunk.

"You ready?"

"As ready as I'm gonna be."

They stepped out of the car and admired the house, which was illuminated very well by the light of the early morning sun. It was a large white house with a red door and red shutters. It reminded Tyler of a clown. There was a two car garage outside and the backyard was fenced in with wood. There didn't seem to be anyone home, and there were no cars in the garage. Tyler motioned for Bunk to follow him and they walked around to the back of the house. There was a latch on the fence which let them into the backyard. The backyard also gave no indication that anyone was home.

"Over here," Bunk called out. He was looking in one of the windows. Tyler walked over and peered through the glass. He didn't see anyone, just a couch, a couple of chairs, and a table with a book on it.

The Book.

"Son of a bitch," Tyler mumbled. "I thought the Creators took that."

"We have to get in there," Bunk announced.

Tyler pulled on the handle to the back door. It was locked. They walked around to the back door of the garage and turned the handle. The door opened and gave them entry into the garage. It was a large room, which didn't look like it had ever held a car. There were no wrenches or rags. There was no oil spot on the concrete floor. Bunk walked over to the door that lead from the garage to the inside of the house and tried to open it.

"Damnit. Locked," he said.

Tyler sighed. He looked around the garage in frustration.

"There is something I can try," Bunk offered. "Give me just a minute."

Bunk glared at the lock on the door and concentrated hard. Beads of sweat had formed on his forehead, and he reminded Tyler of someone who had been holding in a shit for about twelve hours. Suddenly, the metal inside the lock started to vibrate and make small metallic clinking sounds. And then—*click*. The door was unlocked. Tyler was impressed. Bunk looked back and smiled.

"I've done that once before," he said.

They stepped inside the house and realized that they had a bit of a problem. The problem was that the alarm was screaming at them, and Bunk was fairly sure he hadn't mastered turning off security alarms in his mind just yet. Tyler didn't care. He made a mad dash for the table and grabbed the book, shoving it in the backpack he was wearing. They ran upstairs, quickly checking each room for any sign of Ashleigh and not finding any. They ran back downstairs and made a sweep of the rooms on the first floor. Still nothing.

"She's not here," Tyler said to Bunk. "Let's go."

They exited through the front door and ran towards the Jeep. Two police cruisers came roaring around the corner down the street and headed straight for them. Tyler held his hands out in front of him and pushed them apart, causing the two cars to separate and crash into trees on the side of the road. They got into the Jeep and drove away.

"I think I know where to go," Tyler told Bunk. His déjà vu was coming back, but only in small bits.

"How far is it?" Bunk asked him.

"Not far," Tyler replied.

Bunk looked over at Tyler and the bag between his legs.

"So what's in the book?"

Tyler reached into the bag and felt for the small book. His hands found it, and he pulled it out and began looking through it. As soon as he had begun reading where he had previously left off, he heard sirens wailing behind them. Looking in the rearview mirror, he could see a police cruiser was trying to get them to pull over. Tyler reached his hand out behind him and tried to make the police car stop gently. He was trying to get the engine to die, or the tires to deflate. Anything to get them to slow down and stop following them, but the problem was that the cops were shooting at them. Bunk screamed and ducked as a bullet flew through the rear windshield and struck the rearview mirror between them. Glass flew everywhere. Tyler tried to focus. He thought about shooting back, but he wasn't that good of a shot.

Forget being subtle, he thought as he began concentrating on destroying their car, rather than just slowing it. Bunk began speeding up and weaving from side to side.

"I think this is it," Bunk said with sadness in his voice.

Everything was happening so fast.

"What do you mean?"

Another bullet crashed through the windshield, missing both of them. The engine revved as Bunk's foot grew heavier on the pedal.

"The déjà vu," Bunk continued. "I've had it for a while now too. And I think this is it. This is where I..."

Tyler watched in horror as a final bullet struck Bunk in the side of the head.

PART THREE
Same Old Song and Dance

1

The way Tyler felt then, as the Jeep began to roll repeatedly, and Bunk's lifeless body was flying around like a rag-doll, is the same way you feel when you're watching the same movie you've seen a hundred times where the bad thing happens, and you feel like just maybe it will happen different this time, but it never changes. You feel like if you yell at the TV that maybe that character won't die, and maybe even sometimes you forget that they do— even for a while—but they always do. Just like Bunk always does.

The Jeep came to a stop after flipping over a dozen times, and Tyler was thankful for seat-belts. He was sitting sideways, on the side that was in the air. Carefully, he undid his seatbelt and slid down, trying to ignore the immense pain in his legs and chest. He could hear the police car coming to a stop, and doors opening and closing. He looked around for his bag, and saw that it was on the other side of the car, on the bottom, next to Bunk's dead body. But where was the book? He was trying not to panic as he looked around for it. As the officers approached the wreck of the vehicle, Tyler willed all of his concentration into shoving them backwards, and he did with so much force that one officer went through the windshield of the police cruiser, and the other landed on the hood of the car, causing a massive dent. Neither one of them were moving. Tyler's nose was bleeding everywhere, but he ignored it. He had to find the book and get out of there. He could smell gasoline and could hear it pouring out onto the ground. He didn't need to chance an explosion, and all it would take is for one of the officers to get up and shoot the Jeep. Finally, he saw the book; it had flown into the backseat. He stretched out his body as far as he could, reaching for the book. His ribs felt as if they might be broken. With extreme caution, he pulled himself into the back seat and worked his way towards the book.

Small pieces of glass were embedded into his hands from climbing around the wreck of a Jeep. Finally, he reached the book, grabbed it, and exited the Jeep through the hole where the rear windshield once was.

When he got to his feet, he found that he was incredibly dizzy and in a lot of pain. He looked down and saw that he was covered in blood. Some of it was from his hands, some from other small lacerations he had suffered during the crash. A quick survey of the scene revealed that neither of the officers had since moved, the Jeep was a mangled mess, and an ambulance was approaching—among other traffic.

What the fuck.

He quickly shoved the book into has bag and slung it over his shoulder. The ambulance was closer now, only a few hundred yards away. He couldn't afford to let them catch up to him. With much pain, he darted into the woods by the highway, and out of sight. He was sure they had seen him, and would probably radio officers to follow him. As he crashed through the woods, it was tough not to give up. The 9mm pistol in his waistband seemed to call his name. Something about ending his life seemed desirable, like a sweet memory of an old friend.

Nostalgia is a bitch.

He snapped out of it, and realized that he had his hand on the handle of the gun. He quickly pulled it off and shook his head. He heard the loud humming, and his head felt like it was going to implode. He dropped to his knees as blood began to pour from his nose, and the world around him whooshed away.

2

When Tyler returned to consciousness, he found himself in the long corridor again. Things were different this time. Every door was flashing a brilliant blue light. He began to take his first step and swayed as if he was drunk. His footstep echoed with a ripple down the corridor, bouncing off the walls. He reached out to the door closest to him, leaning on it to steady himself as he gathered his composure. He felt like he was breaking down. All of these Variant powers he was using were taking a toll on his physical and mental health.

As he leaned against the door, he thought of Nathan. All of this was to save him—or the entire universe, he wasn't completely sure—but he didn't feel any closer now than when he started. And what was worse was that Bunk was dead.

Dead.

Never coming home.

Tyler felt completely responsible for his death. Even though he knew that Bunk was just doing what he knew he had to do.

Just then, he heard a noise on the other side of the door. It was a scream. Without thinking, he turned the handle to the door and flung it open, stepping out into the night. He recognized the yard and house immediately. It was the yard and house of the late Officer Mills, and it was exactly where Tyler needed to be. For once, Tyler was having déjà vu that was perfectly explainable. He remembered being here before because this is where he was stripped and tortured all those years ago. It was also where he had saved the life of Laura Leigh. It had seemed as if Dugger had continued to use this property for his *operation*.

It was dark outside, and he could see light escaping from the small basement window on ground level. It was the same window that he had seen Laura through the first time he had been here. He carefully made his way over to the window and looked inside. He couldn't see anyone. No sign of Ashleigh or Dugger. He pushed on the glass to see if he could open the window, but he had no luck. He stood up and walked around to the front of the house. The lights were off on the front porch, and he approached the front door, hand on his gun. Something told Tyler that if he turned the door handle, it would open. And it did.

He entered the house and closed the door behind him. If Dugger was here, he would kill him, no question. The first thing he noticed was the smell. The old house smelled of formaldehyde and mothballs. Right now, Tyler was wishing that he had brought a flashlight. It was nearly impossible to make out much more than the shapes of the doorways in the darkness. He took a step forward and the wooden floorboards whined beneath him. Just then, he heard a noise like the squeak of a bed spring coming from a room to the right. It was the bedroom where he found the notebook. He made his way over to the wall and walked along its edge, feeling with his hands while his eyes adjusted to the dark. When he reached the doorway to the bedroom, he heard whimpering and more bed squeaking. There was a cold sweat building up on his forehead. His heart was beating irregularly in his chest. The next thing that happened was a curious thing, even to Tyler. Instead of stepping inside, he had the unexplainable, instantaneous feeling to turn around and shield his face with his arms.

Déjà vu.

A loud crash accompanied a stinging pain as a cheaply made wooden chair broke over Tyler's arms. He yelped in pain and immediately charged forward, slamming his attacker onto the floor. Tyler could feel his Variant powers growing inside of him like a rebellious, untrained circus lion ready to be released. With a surge of confidence, he willed the lights in the room to come on. There was a lamp on the far side of the room which came on with such force that the bulb exploded, but there was the overhead light, and that was enough. Once the lights were on, Tyler saw that the name tag of his attacker said Holt. He had Holt pinned to the floor but he was laughing.

"What's funny?" Tyler slammed his fist into Holt's face and he heard a crack from his nose. Holt winced and snorted before answering

"You think you have a chance. Of saving her. You stupid fuck." He spit in Tyler's face.

Tyler was filled with so much raw emotion. He hated Holt. He hated Dugger. He stood up, simultaneously pulling the Glock out of his waistband and aiming it at Holt's face. There were two things that Tyler saw in his face while he pointed the gun there. The first was that his smug façade was completely gone. The second was that his nose was bleeding profusely. He had to remind himself that Holt wasn't a Variant, couldn't be. A nosebleed doesn't mean the same thing for him. He's not about to bring the ceiling down on Tyler with his mind. Or was he? But something told him *no gunshots—not if you can help it—too loud.* And he didn't *want* to just kill him. Or was it that he didn't want to *admit* that he wanted to? Without giving himself too much time to think, he crashed the butt of the gun into the side of Holt's head, knocking him out cold on the floor. He turned around, not entirely satisfied, but he needed to deal with finding Ashleigh and Dugger. He entered the doorway to the room where he heard the bed squeaking.

When he looked inside, he knew what he would see. It was like the radio stations. Sometimes you didn't know what was going to happen, and sometimes you did. He wished he knew why, but he had a feeling he would know that soon also. But what was on the bed was Ashleigh, tied up with leather straps coming from both wrists and both ankles. Her skin was pale; her eyes white. He turned on the light and she barely reacted, rolling her head to the side.

"Ash..." He whispered through tears.

She didn't reply.

He walked over to the side of the bed where the nightstand was and began working on the straps that held her in place. As he was undoing the strap which held her right arm he noticed the bottle and syringe on the nightstand. They had been drugging her, there was no doubt of that. He worked quickly as he released all of the straps that held her in place. He couldn't help but notice the awful smell, and the stains on the bed. They had been leaving her to shit and piss all over herself. Tyler was making a mental checklist to fuel his rage against Dugger, if the bastard ever showed himself. Finally, he got her free from the straps and pulled her close to him, gently caressing her hair as he called her name.

"Ashleigh......Ashleigh wake up. Please, Ash."

She began stirring.

"Mmmwhat?" Her speech was muddled.

"Babe, it's me." Tyler sobbed. He had lost so much time with her.

"T....Tyler. You came." Her eyes opened slowly as she looked into his, only a small bit of recognition showing on her face.

"Yeah. I'm here," he sobbed. "I'm here to take you home, it's okay."

"Oh. Okay. Thank you." She smiled like a drunk who just told everyone in the bar that she loves them. He was stroking her hair and smiling back at her when he heard a sound which startled him. It was the sound of boards creaking.

"Ashleigh, listen to me, I will be right back. I promise," he stood up and pulled the gun out of his waistband, walking towards the door. She rested her head back on the pillow and passed back out.

He realized immediately upon reaching the doorway that Officer Holt was gone. *This is why I should have ended him*, Tyler thought. He walked out into the foyer again and saw that a light was on on the other side of the house, diagonal to where he was standing. He made his way over to the room, checking back over his shoulder occasionally to make sure no one was entering the room Ashleigh was in. He made it to the room with the light on and saw Holt lying there on the floor, his face covered in blood. It appeared that he had dragged himself in here. The room he had entered was the kitchen. It was a large room, with tile floor and an island in the middle. Holt appeared to be breathing but showed no other signs of life. Tyler wondered if he had turned on the light or if someone else had. But then he noticed something. To the right of the island was a door leading to a connecting room. It was cracked open. It must have been where Holt was headed when he passed out.

Tyler pulled the cell phone and the business card which read **Det. William Dugger** out of his pocket. He dialed the number on the face of the card and waited for it to ring, still keeping an eye on the cracked door. After a few seconds, he heard it ringing, both on his end, and on Dugger's end. He quickly walked around the left side of the island and approached the cracked door. With a loud wooden creak the door crashed open, catching Tyler in the face and nearly breaking his jaw.

3

I'm dead. I failed Nathan and Ashleigh and the whole world because I died, is what was going through Tyler's head as he crashed back onto the kitchen floor. But if there was one thing that reminded you that you weren't dead, it was pain, and Tyler had enough to go around. He shook his head like a dog with ear mites and tried to get back on his feet.

"About time you came running back here boy. I thought your bitch was gonna die before you could witness it."

Tyler reached for his gun, but it wasn't there.

"Looking for this?" Dugger asked him, holding up the Glock. It had fallen on the ground when the door hit him. He took the magazine out of the gun and put it in his pocket, setting the gun on the counter.

"You know," Dugger began, walking towards Tyler. "It's amazing how much trouble you have caused me. This operation was running perfectly smooth until you came along and fucked it all up. And the questioning! Do you know how long it took the public to trust our department after you uncovered Mills?"

"You think that's *my* fault? I'm so sorry that the public wasn't keen on you raping the girls in the community."

Dugger slammed his hand into the cabinet next to him, putting a hole in the wood. "It's not about *rape!* It's about teaching this goddamn community about respect for fucking law enforcement! People have anti police rallies and protests, and here we are, protecting their sorry asses. Someone had to show them what happens when you don't appreciate and accept the help that is offered. We make real differences, you know? We teach real lessons. These people should be thanking us."

"Oh I'm sure they will have their own ways of thanking you after I reveal what you've been doing here in your little torture playground."

"Do you actually think anyone trusts you? Did you forget that you murdered a woman? Kidnapped and probably raped and killed your ex-wife?" Dugger smiled a twisted smile. "Did you forget that you *killed* your own son?"

Tyler was filled with so much uncontrollable rage that he thought steam might start coming out of his ears. He wasn't going to have any restraint like he did with Holt. Dugger was his mistake, what he was supposed to fix, and he was making it very easy for Tyler to find the will to do so. He lunged forward and tackled Dugger, forcing him backwards and through the door behind him. Dugger uttered a maniacal scream, like someone jumping off of a bridge to their death. Tyler landed on top of him in the room on the other side of the door. He looked around for anything to use as a weapon, but the room was dark. But then he remembered: *I'm a Variant.* He waved his hand towards the lights, trying to cause them to turn on, with no luck. Dugger took an opportunity to plant his fist in Tyler's face, knocking him backwards. Tyler lunged forward and pinned both of Dugger's arms down with his knees. He clasped his hands around Dugger's throat and pressed hard on his Adam's apple with his thumbs.

"This is for Nathan," he told him.

Dugger was making harsh choking sounds and kicking his legs, but there was no use. Tyler had him, and he was going to end it. He pressed down on his throat harder, and harder still. Dugger's eyes began to bulge, the veins in them threatened to burst. Finally, Dugger's legs stopped kicking, and his body went lifeless. His eyes remained wide and shocked. He lay there motionless, his dead eyes staring forward like some horrible thing was coming through the ceiling.

Tyler looked around the room, waiting for something to happen—he wasn't sure what—but something. He had done what the Creators wanted him to do, so where was his end of the deal? Would Nathan just magically appear in front of him? He wasn't that naïve, although nothing would seem strange at this point.

He then heard a noise behind him—like something had been kicked across the floor—he glanced around and saw a dark figure standing in the doorframe, watching what took place. It was shaking its head, as if in disappointment.

Creator.

Tyler stood up, hands trembling slightly, and looked down at what he had done. Dugger's face was purple, veins were bulging out of his forehead. It was a grotesque sight. Tyler was surprised and even slightly ashamed that it was so easy to do what he had done. He reached for the light switch and flipped it from down to up, and nothing happened.

He turned away from Dugger and saw that the dark figure was gone. He wanted to shout out for it to come back, to give him his son, but he remembered Ashleigh was still in the other room. He grabbed his gun from the kitchen counter, placed it in the waistband of his pants, and made his way back to her. Officer Holt was still on the floor, unmoved. Tyler kicked him in the ribs when he went by, but there was no response.

When he got back to the room, he found that Ashleigh hadn't moved. He rushed back over to the side of the bed and tried to wake her. "Ashleigh," he called. "Ash, wake up. We have to go."

She stirred only slightly. Waking her was worse than trying to wake a passed-out-drunk friend. Whatever drug they had been injecting into her was doing its job in keeping her subdued. He decided to pick her up and carry her to the bathroom, where he could clean her up. Plus he figured the water might help to wake her. He gently reached both arms under her and lifted. He found that it was incredibly easy to pick her up. She probably hadn't eaten in a couple of days, and she was never all too heavy anyway. Holding her body, he walked carefully to the bathroom across the house. After turning on the lights, he turned on the shower and helped her stand under the water. Finally, she fully regained her consciousness and finished showering herself. After she had finished, Tyler handed her the towel that was hanging on a rack next to him, and she followed him back into the room.

"He put the clothes I was wearing in here," she pointed to the dresser. "He has *a lot* of girls' clothes in there," she said with a shudder.

Tyler admired her beauty as she talked. The way she stood there with a towel around her reminded him of when they were married. She would get out of the shower in front of him all the time, her hair wet and filled with the hypnotizing aroma of lavender, or coconut, or citrus. Even now in her sickly state, she was beautiful to him.

Ashleigh saw Tyler looking at her and she asked, "What?"

"Nothing," he said. "Except, I was wondering...did he try anything with you?" He felt bad even asking her.

"No. At least not that I know of. I spent a lot of time passed out, but I don't think he ever did that…" She was blushing in an ashamed sort of way.

Show me on the doll where he touched you.

"Good…that's good." He didn't know what else to say on the matter.

She reached into the dresser and found her clothes. Tyler turned away and allowed her to dress, a pointless, yet appreciated gesture.

"Is he dead?" Ashleigh's question was blunt and caught Tyler off-guard. He wasn't sure if he was ready to admit it.

"Yeah, he's gone."

"Good."

She was fully dressed now. She approached Tyler with her arms out, and he reached in and hugged her.

"I honestly don't know what to do next," Tyler told her. "My plan to get Nathan back...I don't know if it's working."

"Well what was it, your plan?"

Tyler began to tell her about everything. The Creators, Variants, the mistake he needed to fix, everything. After he had finished talking, Ashleigh was silent as her mouth hung slightly open.

Before she could speak, they heard a moan come from the other room.

"Did you think maybe you needed to kill him too?"

"I don't know. I mean I definitely didn't feel I needed to like I did with Dugger. Usually my...instincts are spot on for these things."

He walked out into the hall, and she followed him.

"I don't know, Tyler. If they were working together..."

"There's no telling how many of them were working together. The others don't matter. Dugger was the one I was supposed to expose, and they'll find him here...there's evidence everywhere. If I kill Holt, I'll have to kill half the police force."

"Then let's get out of here. I don't want to be here any longer."

He nodded and led her to the front door of the house, and they exited into the chaos of the night.

4

Tyler and Ashleigh hadn't even made it to the end of the driveway when they heard it—a loud snap, like a gargantuan tree limb breaking off of an old tree. They both turned around and braced themselves, holding each other as the ground trembled. They watched in disbelief as the house began to cave into the ground. The second story of the house fell down in a V shape, crashing into the bottom of the house. It was as if there was a giant, invisible string pulling the house straight down to hell.

Debris began flying towards them as the earth shook. They turned to run towards the street, dodging deadly pieces of metal and wood. When they reached the street, they turned left. There was a woman three houses down, digging in her car. She was bent over in the front seat like she was looking for something. She looked up as she noticed them approaching, and she spoke directly to Tyler. "It's happening again," she said.

"What?"

"It's happening again," this time she said it with a matter-of-fact tone.

Tyler was entirely sure he had never met this woman in his life.

"What is happening again?"

The woman began to laugh, and Ashleigh screamed for Tyler to watch out, that she had a gun.

"The end of the world," the woman said, and she put the gun in her mouth and pulled the trigger.

5

Tyler's ears were ringing so badly that he almost couldn't hear Ashleigh's screams. He looked behind them and saw that more of the street was caving in, starting with the Mills house. They needed to get moving, and luckily for them, there was a perfectly good car in front of them. It turned out that the owner of the car recently found herself without need of it. The keys were in the ignition, but the only problem was the brains littering the front seat. The woman's dead body was slouched on the ground, leaning against the driver door frame. He grabbed her by the wrist and slung her aside. He found a plastic shopping bag in the backseat and used it to wipe the mess out of the seat. Ashleigh got into the passenger seat, and Tyler cranked the car. He wheeled it around to face away from the destruction that was following them and took off.

"Oh my God! What the fuck is going on?" Ashleigh exclaimed.

"I don't know," Tyler answered. "But I think it has to do with what the Creators told me." He turned right at the end of the street. "They said if I didn't act soon, there would be nothing. I guess I should have taken that more literally."

"But you *did* act. You killed Dugger."

"I know."

"So…what then?"

"I don't know. Maybe Dugger wasn't my mistake." He sighed, his hands were trembling on the steering wheel, partially covered in someone else's blood.

Ashleigh was crying, just enough for Tyler to notice.

"I'm sorry," he said.

"No, I'm sorry. For everything," she nervously shifted in her seat.

"Ash-"

"No, hear me out. It was wrong of me to leave you. Things were just so…fucked up. And I didn't know how to deal with my emotions after dad died."

"I understand."

"But you don't. I'm trying to tell you that I hated you for not saving dad like you did with Nathan.

Even though you weren't there, I felt like you could bring him back. And I know it isn't fair, but it's how I felt."

"Bring him back? What do you mean? And what do you mean like I did with Nathan?" But somehow he knew what she meant.

"See, this is what I mean. It's like you don't know what happened. I was always the bad guy. Every bad tantrum. Every pissy day Nathan had, he took it out on me."

"That's not true."

"Yes it is! He always shared some special bond with you, and I knew I would never have that, because I know how you got that bond. All the doctors said it was best not to talk about it, or bring it up after you woke from your coma."

He turned to face her, the car swaying. "My *coma?*"

"Yes, Tyler. Your coma. You were in a coma for *two weeks* after Nathan was born."

Tyler looked at Ashleigh like she was a stranger. He was hearing what she was saying, but he didn't know how to take it. He pulled the car into the empty parking lot of an abandoned coffee shop.

Ashleigh continued, "When it was time for Nathan to be born, there were complications."

"Preeclampsia, they had to induce you early."

"Yeah. Well you know they had to do a c-section, and when they pulled him out...he was dead." Tears rolled down her face as she talked. She was facing the floor of the car. Tyler just stared, his heart pounding heavily.

She continued, "The doctors were trying to explain to you that there was nothing they could do. That he had lost oxygen to his brain for too long, and you started freaking out. Your nose started bleeding, and there were two doctors trying to hold you down, to give you something to calm you, and right before you passed out...Nathan started crying. You didn't wake up for two weeks. I didn't think about it for some time, I just considered him our little miracle. But one day, I realized what happened. I realized that *you* had brought him back to life."

Everything was coming back to Tyler in a flash. "I do remember," he said. "Oh my God, Ash why didn't you tell me before?"

"Well I saw some doctors—more like shrinks really—who suggested that maybe I shouldn't bring up the fact that Nathan was stillborn to you, seeing as how it caused you to go into a coma. But I knew that wasn't what happened. I should have loved you more for it. But after dad died, I got selfish and asked myself why you couldn't bring him back too. I know it's stupid, you weren't even there. But it's just how I felt, and I'm sorry."

Tyler sat back in his seat, perplexed. Before he had time to gather his thoughts, he had to take action. The ground below the car started to vibrate. He looked in the rearview mirror and saw that the asphalt of the parking lot was cracking and dividing. He put the car in drive and continued in the direction he was heading.

"I don't know where to go," he said.

"I don't either," she replied. "I feel it's less about where we go and more about what *you* do. Do you have any ideas?"

"The book," he said. "Get the book out of my bag."

She grabbed the bag which was in the middle console between them, and began digging in it. The night sky was lighting up with cracks of lightning in the distance, and it began to rain.

"Here, I found it."

"Open it and just start reading. There has to be

something in there about what I'm supposed to do now."

She began reading the beginning, "—now read with a keen eye and we may begin."

"That's as far as I got," he told her.

"That's it," she said. "There's nothing else."

"What? That can't be right. Are there pages torn out of it or something?"

"No."

He swerved the car to avoid a fallen tree.

"Here, take the wheel. Let me look at the book."

She handed him the book and reached over to help steer the car. He flipped through the pages furiously.

"Why would I leave a blank book for myself?"

"Maybe Dugger tampered with it, I mean it does say it doesn't need to fall into the wrong hands."

"I don't know. I doubt it. I think I would have been more concerned with the Creators finding it, but there's nothing in there."

The car started smoking and shaking. He looked at all the gauges, they had plenty of fuel, but it was running hot.

"Damnit, lady," he mumbled. He pulled the car over into the grass when it got to be too hard to see through the white smoke. "Guess we're walking."

Ashleigh got out and held Tyler's bag above her head to shield from the rain. They were on the edge of someone's property. It looked like an old farm-house that hadn't been used for much else other than living space and storage lately. There was a small pond across the road with the ass-end of a car sticking out of the water. There were skid marks leading off the road. They rushed over to see if they could help anyone. When they reached the car, they found a grim scene. There were at least four bodies inside the car, lifeless, and two of them were chil-dren.

6

Ashleigh put her hands up to cover her mouth as she let out a small cry.

"Come on," Tyler said, his voice shaking. "Let's see if these people can help," he gestured towards the farmhouse.

As they walked, Ashleigh said, "D'you know what I thought about a few days ago? Sawyer, when he got run over."

"Why did you think about that?"

"I'm not sure, but I remember I gained a lot of respect for you that day. When you got home from work, you just did what you had to do. He was just lying there in the street, and I couldn't—" her voice trailed off.

"One of the worst things I ever had to do. It was such a mess."

"Well I was thinking, why do things like that happen? Why do puppies get run over, and people starve, and...two year olds disappear from their beds? If God—"

"God? You mean *Creators*? You think they give a *fuck* about our dachshund? They're just like everyone else. They give a fuck about *themselves*. There is no justice in this world that you don't take for yourself." The bitterness in his voice was overpowering.

Ashleigh didn't like this side of Tyler. She was used to the goofy, fun, sarcastic Tyler, but she wasn't accustomed to philosophically depressing Tyler.

"It just feels...wrong to talk about there being no God," Ashleigh said.

The weather had gotten worse. The trees swayed back and forth like lighters during a slow song. The rain came down harder and faster. The property had a white, two-story house, and three barns. They made their way to the front porch and knocked on the door. There was no answer. Tyler tried the handle and found that it was unlocked. He pushed the door open a little bit and called, "Hello? Is anyone here?" There was no reply. They stepped inside the room and shut the door behind them; it was too dangerous to keep standing outside. In front of them was a small room with a TV and a couch. At the end of the room were stairs leading down into the basement.

"That's where we need to go," said Tyler, pointing in the direction of the basement. "But let's check around the house first."

They went into the room on the left and found that it was the kitchen. Tyler opened the fridge and pulled himself out a bottle of water, and he held the door open so Ashleigh could get what she wanted. She reached into the fridge and Tyler went on to check the living room. Still no people. Ashleigh joined him, and they checked the master bedroom and the two bedrooms upstairs. There was no one in the house. They headed back towards the basement, but Ashleigh stopped Tyler as they passed the fridge.

"Here's why you won't find anyone in this house," she said with a sad voice. There was a picture on the fridge of a family of four, posing in front of a car. It was the car in the pond across the street.

"That's terrible," said Tyler, frowning.

They went down into the basement and discovered that it was quite cozy. There were two couches, a TV and a bathroom, among dozens of random knick-knacks. Tyler turned on the TV, hoping to find any information on the state of the world.

Most of the stations were blank. Fox News was one of the stations that was functional. The headline at the bottom of the screen read: **The End of Times.** The reporter was talking to the camera candidly, instead of using the usual scripted dialogue.

"Things are not looking good. We have footage from all around the world showing the destruction and chaos," the view changed to show a tsunami in Japan, and then looting in NYC. *"People everywhere are killing themselves, killing each other. Many of the people from this very studio are dead. I'm afraid to say it, but it seems we are witnessing the end of times."* Static buzzed across the screen, and the picture and sound began fading in and out. Only pieces of what the reporter was saying were coming through.

"—lose signal soon."

"—kiss your loved ones."

"—God help us all."

The screen went black and fell silent. Television was no more.

7

Tyler stared into the blackness of the TV screen in disbelief. He turned around to see where Ashleigh had gone and found that she wasn't in the room.

"Ash?" He called out.

"In here…"

He followed her voice which led him into the small basement bathroom. She was on her knees, seemingly praying to the porcelain gods.

"You okay?"

She opened her mouth to speak, but instead she heaved into the toilet. Tyler rushed over to hold her hair back.

"Get back!"

Confused, Tyler stepped back.

"I was just trying to—"

"But you don't understand. It's happening to me too. I've been fighting the urge for a while now."

"The urge? What urge?"

"I just have this—"

Heave.

"—this powerful desire to…to die. Like the TV said. This must be how the world ends…everyone kills themselves off. How efficient."

Tyler thought out loud, "But it hasn't affected me."

"But you're—"

Heave.

"A Variant," he said, finishing her sentence for her. "I'm so sorry, Ash. I'm gonna fix it, somehow, I will."

"But what can you do? The book hasn't been any help."

Tyler reached into his bag and pulled the book out, examining the cover, the pages, everything about it. It was still as it was before, the cover and introduction page had writing, but the words stopped after that.

Ashleigh flushed the toilet and washed her hands and face. "I'm gonna lie down," she said. "Wake me if the weather gets really bad, or you figure out what we can do."

He nodded as she went to the couch, covering herself with a blanket that was draped over the back of it. Tyler walked up the stairs into the house and looked out the window. The weather was still pretty bad, but nothing life-threatening yet. He went back downstairs, walking as quietly as he could down the creaky wooden boards, and returned to the bathroom where the book lay on the counter. He picked it up once more and whispered the title aloud, "The Man in the Mirror." He looked up into the mirror and dared himself to stare into his own eyes. It was something he hadn't wanted to do since he was a child. Mirrors bothered Tyler. It wasn't that he was self conscious of his looks, (though he was) it was because something happened when he looked too long, something that scared him. He told himself that it was all in his head, and maybe it was, but that didn't change the feeling it gave him.

Read it in the mirror, his inner something told him.

He opened the book and hastily turned the pages to where the text left off and he held it open in front of the mirror. Words danced across the pages in a font seemingly scrawled by hand. The text was large and written sloppily, like someone had written it backwards. There were only four words written in the whole book.

Focus On Your Pupils.

8

Ruth Roydman scolded her son when she picked him up from school on a March morning in 1997. Tyler's teacher, Mrs. Ferguson, had called Ruth at work and told her that she needed to come get Tyler. She said his nose was bleeding, as well as his hands. The blood on his hands had come from broken glass, but the blood coming from his nose was a mystery.

"Why did you do it, Tyler? Why do you have to show out? You know I've been thinking you weren't ready to stop seeing Dr. Hart. You said you were, but then you pull this?"

Tyler sat in the backseat of the Buick in silence. Bandages were wrapped tightly on his hands, tissue shoved in his nose, giving him the look of someone who tried to rob Kevin McCallister's house.

Finally, he spoke, "You don't understand, mom!"

"Evidently not," his mother retorted. "Why don't you enlighten me? Explain to me why you felt it necessary to break every mirror in the bathroom. Jesus, Tyler, we're going to have to pay for that. Not to mention, Susan Ferguson is going to tell everyone we're a bunch of freaks. She already runs her mouth to everyone in Sunday school."

"If she already runs her mouth, then why do you care?" Tyler was quick for a ten year old.

Ruth did her best impression of someone who could ignore such comments, "What is it about mirrors? I just don't get it. You're not ugly, Tyler. I've told you, you're a handsome—"

"It's the man!"

Ruth pulled into their driveway and turned around in her seat to face him.

"There is *no* man," she sounded angrier than she had intended, but she was tired of Tyler telling stories.

"You're wrong!" Tyler said, "I see him. I saw him today. He was looking back at me and screaming."

Ruth and Tyler went inside the house, and Ruth got on the phone with Dr. Hart.

9

The book lay still on the counter as Tyler tried to decide what to do next. He had read the message quite clearly, only he was afraid to do what he knew he needed to do. But when the end of the world was looming outside, you had to act fast.

Hurry, hurry, step right up, end of the world happening right now, whadayuh gonna do about it?

He slowly shifted his gaze into the mirror. There were his eyes, the eyes that changed when he stared too long. And his face, which wrinkled, and his hair that grayed. If he stared long enough, he might see his own corpse.

A loud crash broke Tyler's concentration. He left the small bathroom and found that the door at the top of the stairs was slamming open violently against the basement cupboard. Something had broken upstairs, the front door, some windows, or both, and now the storm winds were pushing inside. Tyler quickly climbed the stairs and pushed against the door, forcing it closed. He latched it with the metallic door latch, hoping it would keep it shut. Water had begun to trickle under the doorway and slowly work its way down the stairs, but it wouldn't be drowning anyone anytime soon. Still, he decided it was probably best to wake Ashleigh. He trotted down the stairs and froze when he reached the bottom step. Ashleigh was still on the couch, but standing over her were three alien-like creatures, Creators. They looked down at her like a child looks at their ant farm.

Fascinating.

"Get away from her!" Tyler demanded.

None of them seemed to hear him.

Tyler picked up an aluminum baseball bat which was propped next to the staircase and headed towards them.

"I said get—"

The creature closest to Tyler turned around and stuck his hand out towards him. Tyler was shoved backwards a few feet, but he managed to keep his hold on the bat, and miraculously, to not fall down.

He charged towards him once more, cocking the bat back like he had just stepped up to the plate at a home run derby. He swung the bat, but he didn't see where it struck because at the same instant, the power went out.

His breaths came in short gasps as he took each step slowly, not knowing where the Creators had gone. He held the bat out in front of him and turned in a circle. Clear.

"Ash," he called.

No response.

Suddenly, the bat was snatched out of his hand, and he let out a small yelp. And then one of them spoke, in that awful whisper voice.

Another human is gone.

Yes, came another voice.

Pathetic, came the third.

"She's not gone...she's sleeping." Tyler said in the darkness.

She's gone. She couldn't handle your failures anymore. The whole world can't handle your failures.

"What are you talking about? You're the Creators, but you can't tell me what I need to do to stop this? I think *that* is pathetic. Don't fucking try to tell me—"

You watch your tone, Variant. Your kind is the reason for most of our troubles. We've been ridding the world of Variants for centuries in order to finally have order. We find that you are the last Variant, and you have caused us much trouble.

Tyler thought back to what Bunk had said about Creators and Variants.

"You can't touch Variants, so how have you been killing us?"

We find our ways.

Bunk, Tyler thought. *The cops killed him, but they must have orchestrated it all. After all, they can affect normal humans. How many Variants have they killed over the years?*

"Where is my son? You said you had him. Why should I fix this shitty world for you if you're just going to find a way to kill me off? And you still haven't given my boy back to me."

Fix it, and we shall see. You don't have long.

Tyler heard a small whoosh sound, and the Creators were gone.

He reached into his pocket and found his lighter. He pulled back on it, and a flame was produced. It wasn't much light, but it was the only light he had. He could see Ashleigh who was still on the couch.

"Ash," he called, shaking her.

Her body was cold.

He turned her over, held the lighter closer, and saw what was lying next to her. He screamed as he picked her up and held her close to him. Nothing was okay anymore. He realized that she had found something in the bathroom medicine cabinet while he was watching the news. The empty bottle of sleeping pills fell to the ground with an earth-shattering, hollow clank.

10

From the diary of Ashleigh Sanders:

April 15th 2015

"I hurt myself today, to see if I still feel."

Okay, okay, I know those are Johnny Cash lyrics, or maybe Nine Inch Nails did it first, I don't know. But the point is, it's true. I'm not proud of it, but I just hate myself for what I did to Tyler. God knows he needs me now more than ever, and I'm just being selfish. Daddy won't come back, there's no blaming anyone. Tyler couldn't...there's just no way. What happened before was a spontaneous thing, and it could've killed him. I think possibly the reason I feel so terrible about it is because I wish I could have done it. But until I met Tyler, I didn't know bringing someone back from the dead was a real thing outside of movies.

Anyways, I felt really stupid after I did it. It seemed like a good idea as I was standing in the shower thinking oh poor me, I deserve this, but when the blood started pouring and the water was causing my leg to sting terribly, I started feeling pretty dumb. I won't do that again. In fact, I don't think I'll ever hurt myself again.

I think I've pretty much decided to get back with Tyler...I know he still loves me.

I just have to work up the courage to call him.

11

In that cool, dark basement, Tyler looked around for someone to help him take the metaphorical dagger out of his belly. *Gutted* seemed an appropriate word for the way he felt. He thought of CPR. He thought of trying to do what he did with Nathan in the hospital, but he knew it would be useless. The Creators said she was gone, and she clearly was. He had the overwhelming feeling, however, that if he could do whatever it was he had to do to find Nathan, then she might live somehow. After all, what would be the point of Nathan coming back if the world doesn't stop imploding on itself? No, Tyler felt certain that he could still fix things.

He was determined. *This ends now*, he thought. He stormed into the bathroom to confront the mirror, to find answers, but there wasn't enough light in the bathroom to see the mirror. He flicked his lighter but it wasn't nearly enough light to see his eyes the way he needed to. He looked down at his feet and saw a small, metal trash can. He thought for a second and left the bathroom, coming back moments later with two old encyclopedias he had found in the basement. He lifted the seat on the toilet and shoved the metal trash can into the watery bowl of the toilet. He then began to tear out pages of the encyclopedias by the fistful, tossing them in, this act of frustration felt good to him. Once the can was good and full, he tossed the spines of the books in as well, and he used his lighter to set the whole thing on fire. It took a moment, but soon the flames were casting enough light across the walls, and he could see well enough to look in the mirror. When he looked in the mirror, he saw that his eyes were red and puffy. He clutched the sides of the sink and forced himself to stare, putting his nose no more than two inches away from the glass.

"Come on," he said, voice trembling. "Here I am."

It seemed like nothing would happen for a few moments, but then Tyler remembered what the book said.

Focus on your pupils.

He concentrated on really looking *into* his eyes,

rather than just *at* them, noting the color, and little dips and valleys in his eyes, bringing to mind the giant eye from *Lord of the Rings.*

Suddenly, it began to happen. The old man began to appear on the other side of the mirror. Tyler realized that it was the old man he had seen before, on the bed, in the library.

"Oh my God," Tyler said. "It's you. It's...*me.*"

The old man turned his head and said, "Are you ready to get your son back?"

"Of course, yes! What do I do? I have so many questions, how are you—"

"You have to hurry. I can't answer many questions right now. But you have to find a way, to get back to that night all those years ago. July 4th."

All those years ago? Tyler thought. *It was only three years ago.*

"You mean like...time travel? Really? How is that even possible?"

"You're a Variant. You've done the impossible already."

Tyler thought for a moment and said, "But you've already lived my life. You have to know how this works, right?"

The old man smiled slightly.

"Like I said, you have to hurry. I know you can do it."

And then he was gone.

12

Tyler reached out and touched the mirror, asking the man inside to wait, to come back, but he didn't come back.

The ceiling above him, which was actually the floor of the first level of the house, began to bow inwards. Water had pooled in the basement floor and was already several inches high. It had to be flooding a great deal outside. He stepped out into the basement and looked up the stairs. The door creaked and threatened to come off the hinges, water poured in at an alarming rate beneath it. He glanced over at Ashleigh's body and felt an incredible pang of guilt, like he was the cause of her death, of the whole world's collapse.

Frustration filled Tyler so much so that he felt heavy with it; it weighed him down like sandbags. He dropped to his knees and began having himself a good old fashioned panic attack.

Stay calm, he was telling himself. *You can't save*

anyone if you're losing your shit.

He remembered seeing something on TV about breathing exercises for panic attacks. Was it breathe in and hold for seven seconds and exhale for five?

Doesn't matter, just fucking do it.

He inhaled through his nose and held it for a while, possibly too long, and then let it out through his mouth. He continued doing so as he pictured the night he last saw Nathan in his mind's eye. It all seemed so vivid, so intense. Nathan was running around the yard with a sparkler. Tyler and Ashleigh's parents were gathered around making small talk, pretending they weren't just there for Nathan. The night air smelled like barbecue and sulfur and freedom. The crickets were making their music, trying their hardest to drown out John Mellencamp on the radio who was saying that life goes on, long after the thrill of livin' is gone.

Tyler hadn't noticed that he was trembling, spilling blood from his nose. He hadn't noticed that he had left the cold farmhouse basement, until he looked up and saw that he was kneeling on his own front porch, on a warm summer night in July.

13

His head hurt, and he tried his best not to puke. Everything seemed hazy, like he was wearing an old, worn out pair of contact lenses. He shook his head, and tried to stand up slowly. His nose was bleeding badly, all over the porch. His head seemed to crack like a fault line was giving way inside his skull. He looked up and recognized his front door, and the porch light was on.

Is this really happening?

He got to his feet—staggering a bit like an Irishman on St. Patty's—and reached for the door.

Locked.

He walked around the back of the house and searched for the hide-a-key, which was hard to do in the dark. Finally, he found it and returned to the front of the house and used the key to enter.

It was dark, but there was enough light from the clock above the stove for him to see where he was going. He moved cautiously, to avoid stepping on noisy toys, and approached the door to Nathan's bedroom. He was nervous, like a teenager who was about to get laid for the first time. His chest rose and fell in an irregular pattern, his muscles were tense. He half expected for Nathan to not be in his crib, for this all to be some sick joke the Creators were allowing to play out. But as he opened the door to Nathan's room, the light from his sleep turtle night light allowed Tyler to see him, sound asleep. Tyler had tears flowing down his face, and he let out a noise that was like a sob mixed with a gasp. He was overcome with joy. He used to come home from work every day and look forward to seeing his little man, and if there was ever a day where he wasn't able to see him, he would be broken up about it. He hadn't seen his boy in over three years, and there he was, sleeping right in front of him.

He turned on the lamp on the bookshelf by the crib, and Nathan stirred a little. He stuck his foot on the release of the guardrail on the crib and pulled the side down. It creaked its 'nails on a chalkboard' creak. Nathan turned over, holding his stuffed Eeyore doll—his Orey—and opened his eyes.

"Daddy!" He shouted with excitement. It was as if he hadn't just seen him a couple hours ago, tucking him into bed.

"Hey bud," Tyler choked through tears.

Nathan got to his feet and reached his arms up in a gesture that said *pick me up*, and Tyler was happy to pick him up. As he held him tight, he sniffed his head and a rush of emotions came over him. *That's where all the good stuff comes out,* he would tell Ashleigh when he sniffed his head, and she would laugh and call him a freak.

But then Tyler heard a thud from the other side of the house, like someone rolling out of bed hard on the floor.

Shit.

He made his way as quickly as he could through the house, and held up his right hand towards the door causing a sort of force field to lock it in place. He heard a loud slam and cursing coming from the other side of the door. Nathan whimpered in the dark. He turned and reached to go out the front door when he heard it.

Shots fired.

The noise of the gunshots startled Nathan and he kicked his legs, knocking over the lamp by the door. They went out into the night, shutting the door behind them. Tyler could hear the sound of breaking glass as the other version of himself climbed out of the bedroom window. He ran around the back of the house and replaced the hide-a-key, not knowing what to do next or where to go.

He will be coming around the back of the house soon, he thought, and made his way towards the tree line.

When they had made it into the woods, Tyler saw them standing there. There were alien-like creatures standing in the woods, waiting for him to approach.

Creators.

He turned around and watched as the other version of himself ran around the house in his underwear, holding a gun. The sight of it reminded Tyler of Walter White from *Breaking Bad.*

He wanted to scream for his help, but he was afraid of what would happen.

Would he be startled and start shooting, possibly hitting Nathan? Would some crazy paradox happen? He couldn't risk it. He turned around as the other Tyler rounded the corner of the house.

Nathan! He heard him yell.

Nathan was confused. He tried to cry out, but

Tyler covered his mouth. He turned to run with Nathan but found that the Creators were blocking his path, surrounding him, even. There were at least a dozen of them, all staring, saying nothing.

"Get out of my way," Tyler snarled. He had come too far to lose like this.

I'm afraid we cannot let you take the boy, the closest one to Tyler said.

"You said I could get him back. I've been through hell trying to get here, you're not getting him."

Nathan whined and shook his legs; Tyler was still holding him on his hip.

Seemingly from nowhere, Tyler was knocked back a few feet and one of the creatures had descended on Nathan, catching him before he hit the ground.

Police sirens became audible, and their lights visible in the distance.

Tyler ran forward and grabbed onto Nathan's arm, pulling him back away from the Creator, who turned, held out a dark hand, and knocked Tyler back on his ass again. The Creator opened up a sort of portal, and they all started stepping into it and disappearing. Nathan called out for his daddy. The sirens were much louder now.

"No!" Tyler screamed and lunged forward and grabbed Nathan again, who was very close to the portal in the arms of the Creator. Nathan was terrified and cried and screamed for his daddy again. Tyler used his free hand to grab a large tree branch close to him, breaking it off, and attempting to hit the Creator with it. Just before the branch struck the head of the creature, it burned up in an instant, and fell to the ground in a pile of ash.

The Creator who had Nathan stepped into the portal, and Nathan started to slip away into the portal with him. Tyler was crying, his nose was bleeding, but this time there was nothing he could do. His powers didn't seem to work against the Creators. Every time he tried to step forward to get a better hold of Nathan, he was pushed back by an invisible force. Tyler's grip on Nathan's arm slipped down to his wrist, and then his hand, until finally, he and Nathan were both holding onto Orey. Nathan looked into Tyler's eyes with such sadness that Tyler thought that look alone might kill him.

Please daddy, no.

Finally, with a terrible, resounding *pop!* The portal closed, leaving Tyler holding half of the Eeyore doll.

PART FOUR
The Potential For
Never And Always

1

He slammed his fist into the damp night earth. He had lost hope, game over. In a fit of rage he pounded the ground over and over like a toddler who didn't get a toy at the store. A mixture of saliva and blood was coming out of his mouth and nose, and he felt like his brain was hemorrhaging.

Why me? What did I ever do?

He let out another intense scream and pounded his fist on the ground, only it didn't strike the ground, it struck water. It had happened so fast, he hadn't even noticed that he had returned to the flooding farmhouse basement.

The water was now up to his knees when he stood up. He waded through it and back into the bathroom to try to communicate with the older version of himself. He was surprised to find that his trashcan fire was still blazing, and he used the light to stare into the mirror.

In almost no time, the old man appeared in front of him, frowning. "It didn't work, I see," he said. "I feared that, but I thought for sure this time—"

"What do you mean, *this time?*"

A loud crash told Tyler that the door upstairs had finally given in, water rushed down the stairs in a roaring waterfall. The old man began to speak but was cut off when the trash can fire went out. The water level was too high, and Tyler either had to get outside and face whatever was happening out there, or drown down here.

Pick your poison.

Tyler moved through the water like an astronaut moves through space, weightless and awkward. It was already above his hips and rising by the second. He grabbed onto the railing on the staircase and worked his way up the stairs as carefully as he could. One slip and his face would hit the stairs, and it would likely be the end of Tyler Roydman. When he reached the top of the stairs, he stepped through the doorway and saw that the front door was no longer on its hinges; in fact, it had smashed through the TV in the foyer. There was water coming in from the intense flooding outside, but it wasn't the only culprit in the basement flooding. All of the pipes in the upper part of the house were busted and pouring water into the house in maddening waves. He stepped outside through the front door, taking one last glance back towards the basement door.

"Rest easy, Ash," he said with a heavy voice.

The world outside had changed dramatically since he and Ashleigh had first arrived at the farmhouse. The sky had turned an ugly bruise colored purplish black, and lightning never seemed to stop littering the night sky like pulses of life on a heart rate monitor. Tyler wondered how much time they had until the world flat lined.

He got back out on the road and continued in the direction they were going before. He just needed to find somewhere dry with a mirror, so he could talk to older Tyler, to find out what to do next. He had so many questions for him.

As he walked, he noticed destruction all along the way. Entire properties burned, livestock wandered in the road due to broken fences. After he had walked up the road for about twenty minutes, he found a Ford F-150 pickup truck parked on the side of the road with its lights on, engine still running. The driver door was open, and when Tyler got close enough he could see why. The driver was lying in the grass next to the truck with a hole in his head; a sawed-off shotgun next to him told Tyler that this was no accident. He climbed into the driver's seat of the truck, shut the door, and began driving towards town.

2

He knew where he wanted to go; he just hoped it was still an option. He tried different radio stations, and found that most of them held nothing more than static. He switched the dial on the radio over to AM and moved through the channels slowly, until finally he heard a voice. It was one of the popular fear-mongering journalists who was saying that he had found shelter and holed up in an old radio tower. He said that the end of times was here people, pray to whatever God you choose. He said that the White House had fallen; the President himself had been part of a murderous rampage, running through the halls and stabbing people with a fire poker. He said most of them were probably so far up his liberal ass that they just let him do it out of service for their party and their country. He went on to say that all major bridges were blocked, filled with the cars of people who had jumped off the side to their death. He said that the Pope had predicted this three years ago, but no one had taken him seriously. What *could* you do anyway, when someone tells you that in three years, everyone would go insane at the same time? How do you stop people from wanting to kill themselves? In the end, it seemed, this was as fitting as any way for the world to end.

It had gotten dark outside by the time Tyler arrived in downtown Monticello, and he was not surprised to find it in ruin and chaos. Gunshots rang out and echoed across buildings and alleyways; buildings were on fire everywhere he looked, and people were looting the ones that weren't. He pulled the truck down a side street to avoid burning cars blocking the main road and saw that there was a man standing in the road in front of him. His head hung down and swayed loosely like someone who had rubber bones. He was wearing a maniacal smile on his face. He reminded Tyler of someone who wanted nothing more than to star in the newest Rob Zombie film. For a moment they were both still, but Tyler revved the engine.

The fuck out of the way.

The man just looked up slowly, still smiling, and

pulled two pistols out of his back pockets. Tyler floored the gas pedal, and the man began shooting. The first bullet whizzed through the windshield, missing Tyler's face by about six inches. The next few bullets were aimed at the tires. The truck slowed as the tires deflated, and Tyler's face slammed into the steering wheel. He got out of the truck, feeling something growing inside him.

The man said, "You feeling lucky, punk?" He laughed and shot at Tyler again. This time, however, Tyler held up a hand, and the bullets turned around, quick as they came, and went right through the man's forehead, dropping him to the ground with a fleshy thud.

Tyler looked at the truck. Both front tires were flat, and there was smoke pouring from the engine, but it didn't matter. He had arrived where he needed to be. The town library stood behind him, untouched. It was funny how nobody tried to loot a library. It was hard enough to get people to read books when the world *wasn't* falling apart, so Tyler felt sure he would be safe here now. He walked up the front steps and tried the door, finding that it was locked.

I just stopped bullets, he thought. *I can open a locked door.*

And he did.

3

He locked the door behind him and looked around the library. Somehow, the building still had power. The lights were on, but dim, like the light cast from a child's night-light. He stepped through the second set of doors and turned right, heading towards the bathroom. He felt the building shake a bit as he walked down the hall, and a couple of pictures fell off the wall.

More explosions.

He reached the bathroom, opened the door, and pulled the light switch to the ON position. An aroma of heavily used urinal cakes mixed with ceiling mold filled Tyler's nose, and it reminded him of coming here so much as a child.

Sweet nostalgia.

Tyler wondered if serial killers ever felt nostalgia over horrible things.

Oh man, that dead animal in the road sure brings back some fond memories.

He walked over to the mirror and gazed into his own eyes, swallowing hard.

Boom, came another explosion outside.

"Come on," he said.

Glass shattered from somewhere down the hall.

"Come *on.*"

Voices shouted down the hallway, *what were they saying?*

KILL THE VARIANT.

"Come on!"

Boom.

KILL THE HERETIC.

"COME ON!"

END THE SUFFERING.

The old man in the mirror said, "If I were you, I'd get moving."

And the lights went out.

4

Tyler backed against the bathroom wall when he saw the door open and heard feet shuffling across the tile floor. It was completely dark inside the bathroom, so he couldn't tell how many people had come in, but he knew it was at least a dozen.

KILL THE VARIANT.

Tyler didn't move.

END THE SUFFERING.

"He's in here," one of them said. "Someone use the flashlight on their cell phone!"

Tyler didn't breathe.

A light came on from across the room, and Tyler didn't give the crowd a chance to come near him. He concentrated, waved his hand, and the sink closest to him broke off from the wall and slammed into the front of the crowd that had gathered in front of the stalls. A few of them fell to the ground, and Tyler used the opportunity to run past them and into the hallway. There were more people coming down the hallway from both directions. He ran instead, further into the library—possibly into a trap—but he had an idea.

I need to get to the corridor, he thought.

He ran to the back of the library, the crowd of people chasing him getting faster and thicker. He found the place where he found the book, where he had met his older self when he was young, and he pictured the corridor in his mind. The corridor with the endless, grand doors.

KILL THE VARIANT.

As the crowd came around the corner, Tyler could see some of them were holding guns; some were holding bats and other random weapons. But it didn't matter; for Tyler, the world was buzzing away as he found the long corridor.

5

"Let me guess," the old man said. "First door you tried?"

The old man was sitting on the edge of his bed the same way he had been when Tyler saw him through the door the last time.

"...Yeah," Tyler said, his voice shaking.

"Yeah. Crazy, huh?"

"Why are all these people following me saying kill the Variant? How do they even know what a Variant is?"

"We'll get to that," the old man said. "Have a seat," he said, gesturing to a chair across the bed.

"No, that's okay. I'll—"

"Sit."

Tyler sat.

"Here," the old man said, handing Tyler a handkerchief. "For your nose."

Tyler nodded and took the handkerchief, placing it under his nose.

"So where do we begin?" Tyler asked.

"We'll begin with the door," the man said. "How did you know what door to open to find me?"

"I just did. The déjà vu—"

"The déjà vu. Right, and that started when?"

"After Nathan went missing."

The old man sat back on the bed, straightening his spine, an audible crack told Tyler that he had popped it.

The old man said, "Everything you know because of the déjà vu, you know because you've done it before. Many times."

Tyler's heart pounded.

"Done it before? How many times?"

"Many."

Tyler shook his head *no,* but he knew it was true. He knew Bunk would die, he knew how to find the book, and he always seemed to know what to do next.

"It hasn't always been easy," the old man said. "When I first started contacting you, we had some...trial and error. But we've made it this far. Sometimes, we don't even make it this far."

Tyler just sat there, not saying a word.

"The mirror thing took me forever to figure out. You know, there is no guide for Variants out there. Although, I guess I could write one. But when you think about it, I sort of did already at one point. Had to end up changing it drastically, using the mirror trick and all, learned my lesson there," the old man laughed.

Tyler was still listening, but he still hadn't so much as opened his mouth. His eyes were wide and unblinking.

"Okay, okay," the old man said. "I can see that I'm going to have to go way back for you this time, that's okay. Are you paying attention?"

Tyler nodded.

"Okay, so you think the story begins with Nathan being kidnapped by aliens."

"Creators," Tyler said.

"Yeah...Creators. Well it actually started before that. When you saved Nathan. See, the Creators had decided already that they were just going to rid the world of all Variants, didn't like the...competition for control and power I guess."

"Yeah, I know that part."

"Well, the Creators didn't like how you used your powers to bring Nathan back to life. He was born dead, and they didn't like that you could change that. They wanted to see you suffer. They wanted you to know who was in charge. Only problem was, they didn't know he was a Variant."

"Nathan is a Variant too?"

"Wasn't supposed to be," the old man said, "and the Creators knew that. The Variant powers have never been passed down through family members like that before. It was always random, keeps things balanced. But when you brought him back, you transferred your powers to him. They didn't know that and—"

"Creators aren't supposed to touch Variants."

"Exactly. The first night they took Nathan from your house, it created a split universe. Think of it like a corrupt data file on a computer. The Creators had broken the rules, had corrupted the data. The world that they knew went on, but it was infected. It was just a copy of the real world, and they would be lost in it. So, time went on in the real world, but then the corrupted world was still there, in the background, causing problems. And now we've gotten to the point where the end of one world can cause the end of the other."

"And I live in the corrupted world still," Tyler

said, frowning.

"Unfortunately, yes," the old man said. He sighed before adding, "Listen, it never gets easier to tell this part. But I'm getting on up in age and sometimes you just don't have time for word games. The truth of the matter is, you've lived the same three years over and over for a long, long time."

Tyler just stared.

"I've devoted my life to helping you try to figure out how to stop it all, not just to end your suffering, but also because when your world collapses, it's bringing mine with it. Each time we fail, you reset back to the day Nathan was taken, but each time it takes a little more out of you."

"And the people trying to kill me?" Tyler asked.

"The Creators can't touch Variants, but they can put whatever motives or thoughts they want to put in regular people's heads. This is usually about the time that they've realized that you can't fix the world by killing that Officer. They think you caused this to happen to the world, and they've given up on getting you to fix it, so they aim to kill you. After Bunk was gone, you were the only Variant left. I guess they figure maybe they can salvage their world by killing the last Variant. When we fail, and the loop resets, people still hate you. Blame you for Nathan, blame you for everything. It's a residual hatred left over from what the Creators told them to believe. It's also why you can stop bullets in mid-air. You've really honed your powers by now."

"That's crazy," Tyler said. "I can't...I just..."

"I'm sorry," the old man said. "But it's true, all of it."

"Do you know what I have to do? To fix it all?"

"Well—" was all the old man could get it out before Tyler was sucked out of the room, suddenly reappearing in the library.

6

"No, no, no!" He looked around in frustration. He was alone in the back of the library which was collapsing under his feet. He ran through the center of the room, dodging falling plaster and brick, and made his way to the front door of the library. The rain had started back, and the lightning was striking often and close.

"What do I do now?" Tyler wondered aloud.

KILL THE VARIANT.

A crowd had started down the street in Tyler's direction. One of them shot a gun at Tyler, striking a tree next to him. Tyler waved his hand dismissively, and the F-150 which was still in the road slammed into the crowd, crushing every one of them. Blood sprayed and smeared the sidewalk and street, and one of the members of the crowd let out a final sentence:

END THE SUFFERING.

7

"Now, I know it's not a popular thing to do..." George Roydman said to his son, "...giving your kids weapons. But it's the smart thing to do." He held up the shiny, new Glock 17, 9mm pistol. "Never know when self protection is the difference between you living and someone else living. And hell, one day you might have kids of your own. You have a responsibility to protect them at all costs."

Eighteen-year-old Tyler nodded. He was standing by his car, which was loaded down with all of his belongings.

"George, he's got a long drive," called Ruth from the front door.

"Yeah," George said, hiding the gun from her, "I know, I know." Ruth smiled and went back inside.

"She doesn't approve, huh?" said Tyler.

George laughed, "What do *you* think?"

"Nope."

"Yeah well, you're a man now. Now look, Glock doesn't have an actual safety, so you have to be really careful. A lot of people think they can disconnect the magazine, leave it hanging out a little bit. But not on Glocks. A Glock will still fire, even with no magazine, long as it's got one in the chamber, understand?"

"Yeah," Tyler said. "Got it." He looked down at his feet and brought a hand behind his head as if to hold it in place. "Thanks dad. Thank you so much."

"Don't mention it."

Tyler hugged his dad, tears welling in his eyes. But he wouldn't allow himself to cry. Never. There was no crying in baseball.

He got in his car and shut the door. He rolled the windows down to let out some of the summer heat, and George called out to him.

"Hey Tyler," he said. "Try not to shoot anyone unless you really have to."

8

He had to find a way to get back to the corridor, to the room with the old man, the old Tyler. He had to have more answers. He tried to *will* himself there, but it wasn't working.

Sorry, we're having some technical difficulties, please try again later.

The wind had gotten so strong that Tyler had to brace himself against the wall of an old building to keep from sliding away. Somewhere far off, there was a buzzing, like in the movies when a plane is falling from the sky. He turned around and looked above the tree line. What he heard *was* a plane falling from the sky, only it wasn't far off.

It was a passenger plane, a Boeing 757-200 with the word DELTA printed on the side, only the side was now pointing down. The plane was turned completely sideways, and the left wing smashed into the steeple of St. Henry's Catholic Church on 7th street, knocking the cross down like some eighth grade kid who listens to too much rock and roll.

This is it, Tyler thought as pieces of building flew towards him. *This is how I die, how the world dies,* is another thought he had as the plane came towards him at the speed of five hundred and thirty-three miles per hour.

There was no more shitty job at the newspaper office. Hell! There wasn't even a newspaper office. There was no more Anne Weaver, no more Bunk, no more Ashleigh. There was no more politics, bills, or Long Island iced teas. And soon, there would be nothing. But somehow, to Tyler, that didn't seem so bad.

I don't care if it makes me selfish, he thought. *Without Nathan, without family, I'd rather there be nothing.*

He put his arms down to his side, closed his eyes, and waited to die.

Boom, he thought. *End the suffering.*

9

So this is it, huh, the afterlife, Tyler mused. *Someone waved the checkered flag, and here I am, finished dead last as always. There are no trumpets here, no huge golden gates, and no Angels, just hardwood flooring and scented candles. Even Hell would be better than this, at least there was a little excitement. But this? This is boring.*

Of course, Tyler wasn't in some version of Heaven or Hell, he was in the old man's bedroom again.

"I'm not dead?" Tyler asked the old man who was standing over him, out of breath.

"I don't think so," he answered.

"Then what happened?"

"I brought you back here, almost didn't get there in time to stop the plane from hitting you this time."

"This time.."

"Yeah, I told you how it works."

"How many times?"

"How many times what?"

"You know, how many times? How many times have we done this, how many times have we failed?"

The old man looked back over his shoulder at Tyler, frowning. "Twenty-six times," he said. "We've failed twenty-six times."

Boom.

"But that would make you...over a hundred years old," Tyler said, shaking his head. "You said it resets every three years."

"Roughly, yes."

The old man backed away from Tyler slowly, "You don't know how hard this has been," he said. "You don't know what it's like helping you over and over, just to watch you struggle and fail. I've dedicated my entire life to helping you, when I really just wanted to break down and ask for *your* help." He coughed a harsh, sick sounding cough.

Tyler watched every move the old man made, the way an antelope eyes an approaching lion at the watering hole.

"What are you saying?" Tyler asked. His face had gone pale, his eyes twitched uncontrollably.

"I'm saying we're getting to the good part, the

part we've never discussed." He had reached the desk on the other side of the room, and he picked up a notebook, holding it up so Tyler could see it. "Everything I've researched, all of our attempts, I've documented here. At first, I didn't know where to begin, but eventually I made contact with you. Sometimes I was able to cross into your universe for brief periods of time, but it was very hard getting the timeline right."

Tyler thought about when he had visited him in the library when he was just a child.

The old man continued, "Anyway, it turns out that you can do a lot of seemingly impossible things when you're a Variant in a universe with no Creators," he rummaged through a drawer in the desk. "Which is what made it so hard for me to accept that there was one thing I could never do." The old man trembled as he pulled something out of the drawer. Tyler could hear him begin to sob.

The old man turned around and handed something to Tyler. "It was so hard chasing you my whole life. I just wanted my father in my life so badly."

Tyler looked down at what was in his hands, it was less than a foot from his face, but it seemed to be a thousand miles away.

It was one perfect half of an Eeyore lovey.

10

Cue music in Tyler's mind, call it a coping mechanism. A particular song starts playing in his head, cymbals crash and reverberate as the guitar picks smooth notes in a cool, repetitious pattern. Thom Yorke sang in his head as his world slowed:

Reckoner,
You can't take it with you,
Dancing for your pleasure

"Dad?"

You are not to blame for bittersweet distractors

"Are you okay?"

Because we separate,
Like ripples on a blank shore

"You're bleeding, snap out of it!"

Reckoner, take me with you

Older Tyler—no—*Nathan* reached down and helped Tyler to his feet. He swayed from side to side as he stood, feeling sick and drunk at the same time.

"Nathan...I'm so sorry," he said as he reached out to hug his son. Tears flowed freely as both of them held each other in silence.

"I'm going to fix this," Tyler said. "I'm going to get our life back."

"I don't know that you can," Nathan said. "I've exhausted all of my ideas; I don't know what we can do. Besides, you need to know something."

"What's that?"

"I've lived a full a life, I'm an old man now. I have kids, grandkids. And I'm tired."

"What are you saying?"

"I'm saying that you've lived the same three years over and over but I've gone on living my life, you know? When they tried to take me, *you* were the one who disappeared in my world. You're the only one. I know it's hard to hear, and it was hard living without my dad, but we made it work. I found out about being a Variant on my own, and I have been trying to save our world ever since. The only thing that's left to fix is..."

"My world," Tyler said. "My world has to end."

Nathan lowered his gaze to the floor, "Yes."

Tyler realized that he was making everything about him, wanting to fix it so that *he* could enjoy a full life with Nathan, not thinking about what that meant for everyone else in the other world.

"But what if I *could* fix it, make it like nothing ever happened?" He said. "You know, we would never know the difference, and you could still have your kids and everything."

"I just don't know how that works. Even if you were able to fix it, I don't know what will happen. The timeline is damn near impossible to predict. But if we don't do something that works this time...well, I'm afraid both of our worlds will end."

"We will find out how it works. I just need you to tell me how to find the Creators."

11

Tyler and Nathan said their goodbyes, and as they hugged, Tyler never wanted to let go. Here was his boy, his baby, never mind the fact that he was now old enough to be Tyler's grandfather, it didn't matter. To Tyler, Nathan was still his silly, amazing, happy little two-year-old.

"Okay," Nathan said, pulling away from Tyler. "I'm sorry, but we have to hurry."

"I know," Tyler said, sniffling.

"Remember, when you're in their territory, it doesn't matter that you're a Variant. They *can* touch you, they can harm you."

"I won't give them a chance."

Tyler glanced around Nathan's bedroom one last time, taking it all in, the pictures on the walls of family he would never meet, souvenirs from places he would never get to visit. It seemed to Tyler that Nathan had led a good, full life. He felt so proud of him and happy for him, but there was still a terrible dread at the bottom of everything.

"Remember," Nathan said. "Find the corridor, go to the end of it. Don't stop or open any other doors; they will try to stop you from getting there."

Tyler told Nathan not to come; he couldn't risk something happening to him. Nathan agreed that in his age and condition, he wouldn't be much help. He was worn down from saving Tyler from the plane anyway.

Tyler stood in front of Nathan's door, and a small smile hit his face. "Thank you for all you've done for me," he said. "I love you."

"I love you too, dad."

Tyler stepped through the doorway and found himself in the corridor one last time. He looked down as far as he could see, and there was no end. There were just hundreds of doors, all lit up, all inviting Tyler to stop in for a peek. He began jogging towards the end of the hall. Doors made noises as he passed them, some of them opening and slamming shut. Some of them would have voices shouting to Tyler as he passed. He put his head down and tried to ignore them. He ran along the corridor for several minutes, still no end in sight. Suddenly, a voice called for Tyler that caused him to stop in his tracks. When he looked up, he saw her, standing in the hallway in front of him. It was Ashleigh. Her skin was a light blue-green tint, like the ocean water looks from far away. Her hair, her clothes, everything was soaking wet. Water pooled around her on the floor, with even more water coming in through the open door she was standing in front of. She reached out a hand towards him.

You can still save me, her voice choked on water as she spoke. *Just come with me through the door, you can stop it, Tyler, baby.*

Nathan was right; the Creators were trying anything to distract Tyler, to keep him from finding them.

Do you even want to save me?

Tyler walked past her as fast as he could, trying to ignore her calls to him.

You're fucking pathetic, you always were, the fake Ashleigh called out.

Tyler began jogging again, to get to the Creators, to get away from the fake woman's screams.

And then another door opened, on Tyler's right this time. He decided to close his eyes, to not even look at what was trying to trick him this time. As he ran past the open door, he felt a small hand touch his pant leg.

Daddy.

"No," Tyler said. "No, this isn't real."

C'mon, daddy. C'mon.

Tyler opened his eyes and saw Nathan in his Ninja Turtles pajamas, moving his hand in the *come here* motion as he called, *C'mon, daddy.*

Just follow me through this door and destroy the human race, is what the Creators were really trying to do.

For a moment, he considered it. He knew it was fake, but he couldn't help it. It was the Nathan he remembered. They knew how to get him. Without giving himself any more time to think about it, he turned away from the fake Nathan, jogging down the hallway, trying his hardest to ignore the cries of *Daddy, please!* He choked back sobs and he was also trying not to cry from the pain in his legs and lungs.

Finally, after what seemed like an eternity, Tyler could see a doorway appearing at the end of the corridor. Slowly, it began to open. Brilliant, white light flooded the corridor, and Tyler had to shield his eyes from the intensity of it.

Suddenly, Tyler felt as if walking any closer to the door—to that blinding light—was a mistake. If they didn't want him to find them, why would they open the door for him? Still, it wasn't like he had much of a choice. Turn around, and he'd have to face the fake versions of his family. Open any door, and the world will end. His only option was to go through the door.

He approached the open door with the caution of a skeptical house cat. With one hand on the frame of the door, he sighed and stepped through the doorway.

12

On the other side of the door, there was a vast
staircase with solid white steps and handrails. It
didn't seem to go anywhere other than up. Up as far
as up goes. He put his hand on the rail and began to
climb. After a while, he began to tire. He told himself that he had to continue on; he wouldn't let the
Creators stop him from reaching them. He pushed
the thoughts of pain and soreness to the back of his
mind and began running up the steps, breathing
harder with each step as sweat poured from his
face, getting in his eyes.

When he finally reached the top, he saw them.
The Creators were sitting in a sort of jury box, facing the stairs, their dark, long figures towered in the
back of the room. Seemingly eyeless eyes watched
him as he approached.

Why are you here, Variant?

"To set things straight," he said.

But we couldn't find you. Why would you come here?

Why would you risk your life, old man?

Just then, Tyler entered the room. He stood in the doorway behind Nathan. "What are you doing? We agreed that I was doing this alone. And how did you beat me he—"

Nathan held out a bony hand in a hushing gesture. "I know what I'm doing," he said as he turned back to the Creators. "I understand that you've told my father that you *had* me. That you used my life as a bribe to get your way." Everything about him was impossibly calm.

Tyler looked at the council of the Creators, to see what their response would be. None of them moved, they didn't even look at each other.

Nathan continued, "You see, you couldn't find me, because I didn't *allow* you to find me."

One of the Creators stood up. Tyler looked at Nathan, and back to the Creator.

"I'm in charge now," Nathan said. "And where I'm from, we don't *need* you anymore. In fact, the world is a much better place without you."

You wouldn't be here without us, the Creator said.

Nathan began walking forward. He walked until he was standing just a few feet away from the stand where the Creators resided. Tyler shifted anxiously as he watched. He began to follow, but Nathan held out his hand for him to stay.

What happened next seemed to unfold in slow motion from Tyler's point of view. He felt so helpless standing there, watching his son, not knowing what to do.

Nathan said, "I think you're mistaken," he shot a glance back at Tyler before continuing, "The truth is, you wouldn't be here without us."

The Creator didn't respond. Its facial expression remained blank. It turned left and right, exchanging emotionless glances with the others. After what seemed like an eternity, it spoke.

We would love to prove you wrong.

Nathan stepped even closer, until he was face to face with the closest Creator, close enough to feel its breath on his face. Tyler began running towards Nathan."Stop! What are you doing?" But Nathan paid his father no mind.

Nathan stared at the Creator with a scowl on his face."Then prove it."

13

One thing Tyler had learned while working for the paper—not that he did any real reporting—was that a lot can happen in a moment. For a reporter to accurately report something, he or she had to be able to observe everything about a specific moment of time. If there was a car accident, it wasn't enough for it to just be an accident between two vehicles. No, it was an accumulation of thousands or millions of decisions, actions, and reactions all occurring within a moment. It was the same for police work, this need for meticulous scrutiny and attention to detail. If Tyler had been asked to report what happened next, however, he wouldn't be able to speak at all. He would be so stricken by the absurdity, had he been questioned. But of course, there would be no questioning; there would be no time for that. What happened was that the Creators took Nathan up on his offer, to *prove it*. In truth, a better way to put it would be that they fell for his trick. Tyler realized what was happening before it happened. Before Nathan pulled an old copy of the ROYDMAN book out from under his shirt and flung it at Tyler from across the room. Before the Creators all stood in their place, placing their hands to their temples, causing Nathan to fall to the ground, writhing in pain. Before Nathan's heart stopped, and before he opened the book and read the writing on the first page. It wasn't that this had happened before, it couldn't have. It was just that it suddenly made sense to him, as if Nathan had gotten into his head somehow and planted the idea. While opening the book, he turned to the first page and confirmed his belief by reading the words:

If there are no Variants, there can be NO Creators, these are the rules.

Everything was happening so quickly. Tyler screamed at the Creators, cursing them. He knew that it was Nathan's intention to have them kill him, but it didn't make watching his son die any easier. He shouted to the whole room, "Don't you know what you're doing? I'm the only Variant left!"

And some Variant you are, can't even figure out your mistake. Can't even do your job.

"You still don't get it, do you?" He said to them. "This is all your fault! If you hadn't tried to take him away," he pointed to Nathan's lifeless body. "Then none of this would have happened!"

He was a...problem...that needed handling.

Tyler's temper was escalating to unsafe levels. If these creatures really were the Creators of the world, how could they be so dense? He looked down at the book again and read the message Nathan had written for him. He knew what it meant. A part of him had always known what he would have to do to end the cycle.

He reached his arm behind him, feeling for something in the small of his back. He wrapped his fingers around the cool metal of it and pulled it around the front of his body. He had actually forgotten it was back there. It had been there since he left Mill's house. It was the Glock 17 his father had given him. There was no magazine in the gun, he had forgotten that in Dugger's pocket, but there was still one in the chamber. He always left one in the chamber.

One of the Creators said, *your human weapons cannot harm us.*

Tyler half-smiled as he looked down at the gun in his hands, he held it like a toddler would hold it if he found it in the street. It felt foreign to him, like he had never seen one before. Maybe it was that Tyler was trying to get extra acquainted with it, the way you do with someone on your first date, feeling out the situation, wondering if and when to sneak in the first kiss. He turned it over in his hands again, and finally, placed it in his right hand and turned it towards his right temple.

"I think it *can* harm you," he said.

NO! The Creators all shouted, moving towards him as quickly as they could.

Tears ran down Tyler's cheeks. He thought of everyone he would never see again, even if this worked, the chances of him living on in Nathan's universe were very small. He thought of Nathan. He thought of Ashleigh, his parents, everyone. Finally, he thought of his father, who gave him the advice: *try not to shoot anyone unless you really have to.*

"Sorry, dad," he said aloud. "I really have to."

And he pulled the trigger.

14

The sun crept through the windows one warm June morning. The wallpaper transformed from dull grey patterns and shapes to a light shade of blue, as the room illuminated. The light danced across a banner which read Monticello High Football. The light stretched further, reaching a dresser which held socks, underwear, shorts, tee-shirts, and an unopened and very much unused box of condoms which were hidden, only not very well. The light continued on, until it finally reached the desk in the corner of the room.

The contents of the desk were: school books, folders, papers, writing utensils, a pack of gum, a Minnesota Twins game ball and a small amount of marijuana which was hidden a bit better than the condoms. Overall, it seemed not too different than the bedroom of any typical high school senior, except for the folder on the desk which was left open about halfway. There were notes scrawled all over it. Different years were listed in random places. 2016, 2032, 2069, 1994. At the bottom of the page there was a note saying *this time will be different.* The words, *time travel?* were written in another corner. More seemingly random notes were scrawled. *The library. Maximum amount of times? One can live without the other. Change the book. The timing probably won't be right.*

Suddenly, the alarm on his phone sounded off. It was a spacey song called Dayvan Cowboy. He found out about the band Boards of Canada through his father's record collection, which was, in reality, now his record collection. He rolled over in bed, his mess of hair stuck to his forehead and picked up his phone. He swiped his finger to the right to stop the alarm. His mom called from the hallway.

"Come on, Nathan. We're going to be late for the tour!"

"I'm coming, mom," he said.

He stood up, stretched, and threw on some clothes. Turning to head out the door, he picked up a brochure which had University of Minnesota printed on the cover. He stepped out into the hallway and heard a knock on the front door.

"Hey, will you get that?" Ashleigh called from the bathroom. A cloud of hairspray threatened to choke her to death.

"Yeah, yeah," he said, sighing and brushing a hand through his hair.

He walked to the front door, sliding the deadbolt and unlocking it. He opened the door and stood quietly for some time. His mouth opened and closed, his eyes unblinking.

"Who is it?" Ashleigh called from the bathroom, but Nathan hadn't heard her, not really.

He smiled.

The End

Justin M. Woodward began writing this book on
12/08/2015
And finished on
07/28/2016

About The Author

Justin M. Woodward lives in Headland, AL with his wife, Alison, and his son, Nathan.

I won't be the guy who tries to tell you that I was always going to be a writer, but I do remember from early on that it was enjoyable for me. I was always the kid walking around with the latest *Goosebumps* book. There is one instance I can recall with decent clarity, which might be the first work of fiction I attempted to write. I was probably nine years old, and I told my babysitter (whose face and name I can't really remember) that I was going to write a book—a horror one—and I needed her help. I would tell her what happened and she would write it down, enthusiastically.

A couple of years later, I had become obsessed with the *Scream* movie series, and decided (long before it was reality) to write a screenplay for *Scream 4*. I didn't know what fan-fiction was but I had written a decent piece with twists and turns. I felt accomplished.

Somewhere along the way, I descended into adolescence and adulthood. Writing stories wasn't cool anymore, not that I have ever really been concerned with what is and isn't *cool*, I just mean to say that it didn't interest me in the same way.

I became a musician and played with a few bands and realized that I enjoyed that kind of artistic expression. That's why I couldn't understand cover bands. I liked being original and playing the shit out of original music, whether a hundred people showed up to the show, or three people, as long as *someone* enjoyed it, I was happy.

Last year I realized that I had a passion for writing original stories. I would have an idea come into my head with such intensity that I had to write it down somewhere. The first story I thought of would eventually become *The Variant*.

The story of *The Variant* originally came into my head while I was listening to a song from Josh Eppard's rap project, Weerd Science. Josh is the drummer from Coheed and Cambria, a huge part of my life for the past ten plus years. His group, Weerd Science, made a trilogy of albums, aptly named *The Illogy*, and the premise of unknown visitors coming in the night (which was a central theme of the "Red Light Juliet" trilogy) stuck with me. And so I created this story while throwing in heavy doses of my own personal experiences (yes, I even put my child in the story, name and all) but as Josh says in another Weerd Science song, "They say to write about what you know about." It just felt right for this particular book to hash out some things I was dealing with in the best way I felt necessary. The writing was therapeutic for me, and I enjoyed every minute of it.

I wrote this book in stolen moments while still holding down a job where I work 50-60 hours a week, as well as chasing a two year old around. I'm not a hero, I know, but it feels good to accomplish *anything* when you have the kind of schedule I do. I wrote a large portion of the book on my phone while riding in a truck at work.

I will begin working on my next novel soon, and I can't wait to hear from all of you about this one. If you enjoyed this book, please write me a good review on Amazon and Goodreads. Tell your friends about it, but just know that if you enjoyed it, then my job is done here, because as long as *someone* enjoyed it, then this show was well worth it.

-Justin

© Copyright 2016

Justin M. Woodward, simple bicycle publishing

www.ingramcontent.com/pod-product-compliance
Lightning Source LLC
Chambersburg PA
CBHW031701170626
46808CB00005B/1563